THE OPERATOR'S MANUAL FOR PLANET EARTH

Also by D. Trinidad Hunt

•

Learning to Learn:
Maximizing Your Performance Potential

THE OPERATOR'S MANUAL FOR PLANET EARTH

D. Trinidad Hunt

Printed in the United States of America.

For information address Hyperion, 114 Fifth Avenue,
New York, New York 10011

Library of Congress Cataloging-in-Publication Data

Hunt, D. Trinidad.
The operator's manual for planet earth / by
D. Trinidad Hunt.—1st ed.
p. cm.
ISBN 0-7868-6177-0
1. Conduct of life—Fiction. I. Title.
PS3558.U46795064 1996
813'.54—dc20 95-38674
CIP

First Edition

1 3 5 7 9 10 8 6 4 2

This Book
Is Dedicated to
All the Parents
on Earth
That By Their Understanding
Life Shall Be Easier
for Both Themselves
and Their Children

•

And to
All the Children
of Our Planet

•

May Your Life Journey
Be the Sacred Adventure
That It Was Meant to Be

For my mother and father
Whose guidance and counsel
Encouraged and supported me
During my early years
Your love is always with me

•

Thank You

Contents

Acknowledgments

Although this book was started on a mountain top, it was not completed there. It reached its final stages in the heart of the city and in the midst of business as usual. The story of the miracle that surrounds it is the story of people. Delivered on the wings of love, this book was supported in the hearts and minds of friends and family who continued to encourage us throughout its different phases.

Thank you to our entire family of over sixty people at Hawaii Business Equipment. Your spirit lingers between the pages of this book in all things large and small that you contributed so that I would have time to write.

To our dear friend Renee Gomes. It was in your cabin that the original fifty pages of this book was written. Thank you for your commitment to the vision and for the countless stream of little things that fill in all the spaces of our every need.

Thank you to Michelle Jerin. Your support in the initial editing stages of this book and your belief in its message often inspired us to keep going.

To Betsy Bowen for her help with the original manuscript, and to Rolinda and Lovell Harris, Jackie Taylor, and Jocelyn Pratt, the team for whom the

Academy Élan was founded. Thank you for the role you played in our lives.

Thank you to the people at the Kona Surf. You always went out of your way to insure a special space for us to write. And a special thank you to Craig Neddersen, Mary Villaverde, and Kalili Murayama for all you did to make our visit perfect.

To our dear friend, literary scout, and agent, Chandler Crawford, who stepped through the pages of destiny with us. Thank you for all that you give out of who you are. Our love for you is immeasurable and transcends time. Carol Fredrick, thank you for supporting us through all of the stages in this work. Thanks, Peter, for helping us get the book off the ground in Maui. And thank you, Fred. Your tireless support is always felt.

To my dear editor, Lauren Marino, without whom this work would never be what it now is. Thank you, Lauren. Because of your guidance and counsel the finer details of this message have come to light. Thank you to Laurie Abkemeier who became the book's surrogate mother and who loved and cared for us through its release. A special thank you to our support team at Hyperion—Bob Miller, Brian DeFiore, Lisa Kitei, and Karen Gerwin-Stoopack—who paid attention to all the little details of production. And thank you to all the people behind the scenes at Hyperion who helped carry this book through to completion.

Thank you also to our Canadian family—Pat, Juoy, and Uncle Moe—who supported us in every way when I had to retreat and write while I was on the road in Canada.

Thank you Jacque Parkinson, for taking care of our every physical need in the final hectic stages of editing.

To Jamie Oshiro, Sheryl Sakuma, Colleen Manke-Davis, Lester Higa, Diane Takushi, Sandy and Bill McRoberts, Stephanie and Chiyoko Mew, and Faith Geronimo, and to all the rest of you who stepped in at the final hour. Thank you for your courage and unwavering commitment to the vision of a new world for our children and our children's children.

To Michelle Noelani and the endless list of friends and family whose love and support was felt throughout the years. Thank you for every phone call, every word of encouragement, and every note. I hope that you know how much your loving gestures nourished and sustained us in this work.

I am also especially grateful to my grandmother, who delivered the seeds of this teaching to me shortly after she passed away.

And finally, to the person who is the "we" and "us" throughout these acknowledgments. Thank you, Lynne Truair, for running the other 70 percent of the company, for filling in all the missing pieces, and for being who you are. This book belongs to the spirit of you and of our work. May its message reach out into the nooks and crannies of the world, bringing hope, light, and a renewed sense of purpose to all it touches.

THE OPERATOR'S MANUAL FOR PLANET EARTH

PROLOGUE

Rhea's students were bothered. The world seemed such an insecure place. With terrorism in Europe and the Middle East, starvation in Africa, and now the civil unrest on the North American continent, young people everywhere felt threatened.

Anxiety knocked on the neighborhood doors in the form of AIDS, gangs, and drugs. Neither parents nor teachers could fully allay their fears, for children were facing adult choices. Students expressed their insecurities in a multitude of ways: some exhibited marked signs of withdrawal or apathy; others were aggressive or even angry; while a good 10 percent of her class revealed symptoms of attention deficit disorder.

Rhea felt sorry for the plight of the world, but she was even more concerned with the plight of the children. She knew they wondered where they fit in the scheme of things, or if they fit at all. She wrestled daily with the question of meaning. How could she help her students find certainty in an uncertain world?

Rhea had a recurring dream. She saw herself standing alone in a room. Directly in front of her was a curtain covering a window. Suddenly the curtain parted. A figure formed in the mist that swirled beyond the window. She was tall and delicately proportioned with dark eyes and straight, shoulder-length dark brown hair. She was wearing a floor-length ivory-colored robe, and Rhea was immediately struck by the aura of peace that surrounded her. The woman was carrying what appeared to be a rock in her hand. As Rhea gazed at her, the rock cracked open and a stone rolled out. It came to rest on the floor about three feet from the window, and as it did Rhea could see the word PURPOSE *written on it.*

The light in the woman's eyes filled with tenderness. "Purpose is missing in the lives of our children," she said. Then she disappeared, slowly dissolving into the mist.

Immediately the scene changed, and so did the energy. Now there was a room just beyond the window. There were people in the room putting on space suits, methodically, one by one. Finally the room beyond the window and the window itself would always disappear, and Rhea would find herself standing alone in her own bedroom.

There were lights in her room: clear, bright, floating lights that resembled beautiful colored jewels. Soon, bodies of various shapes and sizes would appear. They hung lifeless in midair. Finally, the jewel-like lights would enter the bodies. For a moment the eyes would flash with extraordinary brilliance, then the lights would disappear within the bodies and the eyes would darken. Only bodies could be seen after that. Now they were alive, animated, walking, talking with each other as they moved through the room.

Night after night Rhea had this dream, and night after

night she would wake up sweating. She knew that purpose was the key, but there was more to the message than that. What did it all mean?

One day, when Rhea could no longer ignore the anxiety in the unresponsive eyes of her students, something inside her snapped. She moved out from behind her desk and began a monologue. As she spoke her words became more intelligible and their spontaneity surprised her. She seemed to be repeating what happened in her recurring dream.

"The human body is a like a space suit," she said as she tapped her shoulders referring to her body. "We put it on when we enter the Earth." She dropped her arms as she continued. "The only difference between our body suits, and the suits they wear in space is that we haven't been trained on how to use them."

The students were puzzled. Rhea could see the bewilderment in their eyes. She coaxed them slowly, deliberately. "When astronauts receive their space suits they also receive a rigorous training on how to operate them. At the same time they receive an operating manual along with the suit, so that if anything goes wrong out there they can troubleshoot and correct it.

"In other words, when we come to Earth it's just like being an astronaut," she continued. "We have to put on a suit in order to live here."

The students were still perplexed but no longer

distant; they were curious now. Rhea smiled and her voice lightened. "You haven't seen anyone walking around without a body, have you?" A nervous laugh rippled through the room.

"The only difference is that we didn't get a manual or training when we got our body. Because of this we've lost our sense of purpose and forgotten why we're here. If we had a manual we could just go look it up whenever we were confused about our lives."

She had to penetrate their listlessness.

Moving closer to the group, she pressed on. "Don't you understand what I'm trying to say?" Her tone was compelling yet emphatic. "You are special," she said. "You came here for a reason. Your body is on loan to you for the duration of your visit on Earth. When you leave you have to turn it in."

The apathy in their eyes began to soften now.

"Life isn't just a random event. There are no accidents. Each of you is here for a reason.

"There is a goal," she continued. "There is a purpose to be accomplished while we're here on Earth." Rhea could see a light in the children's eyes now. She recognized it. It was the same light she'd seen enter the bodies in her dream. Perhaps she could help them after all, and in doing so she could also help herself.

Chapter 1

Beyond the Window of Time

Élan closed the door behind him as he entered his sleep chamber. Placing the manual on his night-stand, he walked over to the window and opened the curtain. Clouds swirled in misty white wisps that parted now and then, just long enough to catch a hint of blue beyond. Élan leaned into the window enclosure and pressed his forehead against the cold pane to stare into the vapory haze. It was always the same, always impenetrable. How he wished that for just one moment he could pierce the foggy ethers to catch a glimpse of the world beyond. Rhea was already in that other world. She had left several birth waves earlier, and he longed to see her.

"Soon it will be my turn to pass through the window," he thought, pushing himself up from the window ledge. He wondered what it was really like on the other side of the Window of Time. Even with all he'd learned in this morning's training session, he was only beginning to understand the distinctions. One was a timeless world of light and energy; the other was a world of solid matter. One was a world of vibration where thought traveled at the speed of light. The other was a world of density where things happened in time and according to sequence. The two worlds were so different.

Walking over to his bed, Élan sat on the edge, purposefully grasping the side of the mattress. Closing his fingers, he squeezed tightly in order to feel the sensation of a grip. He watched in awe as the veins in his wrists popped to the surface. This experience of dense matter was so new to him. Before this morning he had never worn a body nor experienced weight. Now, because of the plan, he was experiencing both. Clenching his hand again he watched his knuckles turn white as the tension ran up his arm. "Amazing," he thought. Releasing his grip he turned his right hand up and stared into its palm. It was etched in lines and creases.

At that moment he caught a glimpse of the manual. Reaching over, he lifted the book from the nightstand, immediately aware of a tingling sensation in his arm.

Lying back with the book on his chest, he propped his head up on a pillow, trying to recall what he heard about the plan. In his wildest dreams he couldn't have plotted a better strategy. Earth was in trouble and drastic measures were needed.

Élan flashed back. Images of early morning drifted before his inner eye. He was in the training room just before the plan was unveiled. No one had received a body yet. They were still pure light . . .

• • •

"Welcome to the Planetary Briefing Room," Elder Em's light flashed in the center of the room. "I'm sure all of you are wondering why you've been summoned here."

Élan was curious. Elder Em was a member of Earth's Planetary Welcoming Committee, a body of beings responsible for guiding the awakening of consciousness on Earth. For thousands of years the Committee had been working to assist souls in their development. For this meeting to have been called by one of their members in such an unusual flurry of excitement meant that something unusual was happening.

The elder continued. "Years of preparation have led up to this moment. Earth is in trouble. Drastic measures are needed. I represent the Committee when I say that we can not afford to let another generation of souls be born without an intervention. Our goal is singular, our purpose intentional. Thus we have created a bold new plan for the rapid evolution of consciousness on Earth."

Élan was stunned as he scanned the energy in the room. Zendar's presence was evident as they mentally connected. Had they heard the words correctly? Were they really involved in the plan?

Élan returned his attention to the elder as he continued, "The initial stage of the plan consists of three parts. The manual, the training, and the simulations."

Élan watched intently as the elder's light moved to the front of the room. He'd been with this beloved mentor for an eternity. There was an unspoken bond between them. "We'll take the plan in stages," the elder continued. "We are about to begin with the first stage, the introduction of the operator's manual for planet Earth."

As the elder spoke, a beautiful holographic image materialized in the air above them. It was a book of soft teal with luminous silver letters on its cover that read:

What Does It Mean
To Be
A Human Being?

"So this was the manual they were talking about," Élan gasped, as he flashed back to a vivid scene sometime earlier . . .

Moving hurriedly through the empty corridors of the training complex, Élan suddenly came upon two of the elders in quiet conversation. "The manual is almost ready," whispered one of them.

Startled by Élan's sudden presence, the elders hesitated in their conversation, then moved along.

At the time it had felt strange, but in his haste Élan had forgotten it until this very moment. "The two elders had been very secretive," he thought. But, because he was distracted at the time, he'd assumed they were referring to something ordinary. He realized now that this was the manual they were talking about. He wondered what message it carried.

"The manual holds the secrets for a successful life on Earth," said Elder Em as if confirming Élan's thoughts. "Let me explain."

Élan watched intently as the elder continued. "Until very recently, the trial and error method of learning has been used almost exclusively on Earth. Because it was created during another time, it was based on the learning style, 'If at first you don't succeed, try and try again!' "

Elder Em's light flashed in Élan's direction. "Although valid, this method is extremely time-consuming. Our new approach is simple and direct, a way of instruction, visualization, and application." He paused, silently observing the room. "As you know, birth is coming soon, and you'll want to get the most out of the training before you start your journey."

No one had anticipated this. Every other birth wave had left for Earth without training of any kind. Ashley's interest was aroused. "Will it replace the trial and error method?"

"Not completely," Elder Em replied. "As you know, Earth has always been referred to as the planet of free will. As a result of their free-will policy, souls on Earth can choose to develop at any rate they desire. However, this new program will serve as an alternative method for the more dedicated students."

Elder Em was obviously enthusiastic. After all, he had been part of the planning committee that had spearheaded the project. "It will give the more determined souls an opportunity to accelerate their development."

"How does it work?" asked Zendar, as if speaking for the group.

Élan smiled to himself. He appreciated Zendar's inquisitive nature. His friend was ever curious, tenacious in his search to understand the meaning of things. This quality seemed to represent his name, which stood for deep reflection and courage to seek the truth.

"Three simple steps," answered Elder Em. "Step one . . . READ the first portion of the manual; Step two . . . MEDITATE on each lesson, committing it to memory. Step three . . . PRACTICE . . . We are preparing an Earth simulation in which you'll have a chance to test what you've learned. Then we'll repeat the cycle: read, meditate, practice, until all the lessons are fully absorbed."

Elder Em was pleased with the opportunity to finally test the plan after years of preparation. "Success on Earth will depend on the strength of your intention during training. The timing of each of your personal awakenings on Earth will occur in direct proportion to your willingness and desire during the training program."

Élan felt relieved. He had been sure that his desire

counted for something, but although firm in his resolve, until this very moment he'd had no validation regarding the power of intention. He wondered about the other souls who'd been born without the manual or training, especially Rhea. She was such a spirited soul with strong intention. She had once shared her dream of being a teacher with Élan. Élan hoped she had found fulfillment.

The elder's voice slipped between his thoughts, drawing Élan's mind back to the discussion in the room. "We need to give you some further background information on the physical characteristics of Planet Earth before you go to your sleep chamber to begin your reading."

As he spoke the book dissolved in the ethers. It was instantly replaced by a stunning holographic blue-green image of the Earth. Elder Em's light shimmered. "This is what you've all been looking forward to," he said. "This is a light image of Earth, your soon-to-be home.

"Earth is made up of large land masses and oceans," Elder Em continued, his tone reflecting his obvious love for the planet. "In fact, there are seven major continents on the planet separated by vast stretches of open sea."

Elder Em began highlighting the various sections as he spoke. "Two-thirds of the Earth is water." Everyone was in awe as the Earth began to slowly rotate in midair.

"What do you think?" he asked. His voice now seemed to hover in the atmosphere like the Earth above them.

"I think it's fantastic!" Élan found himself whispering. He was amazed. It was beyond anything he could have even imagined.

"Are those its real colors?" Brooke's voice came from the back of the room.

"Those are its real colors," Elder Em responded reverently.

"It's stunning," Jaron murmured under his breath.

The entire class was enthralled as the elder gently unraveled the mysteries of Earth. They asked one question after another as he spoke of the differences in the regions and the weather. Images synchronized with his words to clarify the teaching. They saw differences in terrain as the North Pole appeared and then dissolved into the European coastline. They traveled the waterways and felt the climatic changes as he helped them distinguish between one area and another.

Their three-dimensional journey took them through the Earth's history as the Elder spoke of the many changes that the planet had been through over the ages. As he described the vegetation each item appeared and aroma filled the room. They smelled jasmine and pine, eucalyptus and rose. Then, one by one, the animal kingdoms were introduced to the group. They saw the creatures of the sea and heard the whales' song. They watched as gazelles gracefully leapt across the African grasslands and plains.

As their journey came to a close, Justin called out. "So what about human beings? What makes human beings different from the animals you showed us? Where do they fit in the scheme of things?"

"The thing we're really interested in, Elder Em," added Zendar, "is what kind of bodies we'll be wearing when we get to Earth."

Elder Em had been anticipating the question for some time before it came and was ready with an answer. "Human beings are very special," he said. "As you've probably guessed, they have a unique place in the scheme of things."

With a flicker of light, the Earth vanished. It was instantly replaced by two bodies, both male and female, clothed in form-fitting violet outfits. A silence more profound than any before resonated in the room. Each soul's heart was struck by the awesome beauty of the physical forms that hung in the air before them. "This" whispered Elder Em just above the silent thunder in the room, "is the human body." His pause was purposeful now. "It is a replica of the body suit that each of you will be wearing when you live on Earth."

Élan was spellbound. So this was what the human body looked like. He had often wondered about it, but he'd never been able to envision three-dimensional space. In his wildest dreams, he could never have imagined anything so beautiful as this. The rest of the room must have felt it too. Nothing broke the silence for a long time.

Finally, the Elder began to speak. "The human body comes in two forms, male and female," he said. "And it is the most highly developed on Earth. None other can compare to its refinement, elegance, or grace." As Elder Em continued, the legs of the holographic figures began to stretch and stride and step in air. "No other physical form is of such flawless design, for it was made to be able to perform the most intricate of movements."

All were mesmerized by the fluid moves of the bodies as they performed the subtle and soft turns of the pirouette and then the powerful leaps and jumps of a running stride.

Shifting their attention to the upper torso, Elder Em continued. "Notice the rotation of the arms, allowing for maximum stretch and reach." At that moment both figures raised their arms and began to move them in a complete circle. Soon the circular motions stopped. The figures stretched, slowly reaching in unison as high as they could. Then they bent and touched their toes in the air. It was a perfect demonstration of the full flexibility of the trunk and upper region of the human body. The over all effect was an elegant but simple dance elucidating the power and suppleness of the human form. The students marveled.

"Now, let's look at one of the most distinctive features of the human body: the human hand." As he spoke Elder Em directed the group's attention to the hands on the forms before them. "The human hand is the most functional hand on the planet. It is the only one that has what is known as prehensile grip."

As he spoke the lighted images turned and faced each other. Gently reaching to span the space between them, they took each other's hands. Bowing slightly, they spun away from one another and held their hands up for all to see the delicate movement of the wrist as they opened their palms, reaching upward into the air.

Then each of the lighted images showed how the thumb and first finger worked together. In slow motion, they moved their index fingers toward their thumbs, until they met. "Notice this perfection in structural design," the elder said, gesturing toward the figures above his head. "The human hand is capable of holding things, and it is this ability that has set it apart. Prehensile grip has given human beings the capacity for delicate movement and intricate manipulation. Because of it human beings have been able to create and use tools that allowed them to surpass all the other species on Earth."

Instantly, the forms disappeared and Elder Em's light spiraled in the air and dissolved. The entire class gasped. At the center of the swirl of energy he materialized in three-dimensional form, wearing a human body suit. He was wearing a violet form-fitting outfit identical to the ones in the demonstration. His soft green eyes, accented by a head of stunning shoulder-length silver hair, looked almost translucent. Extending his arms, he duplicated the movements that the figures had demonstrated with their hands minutes earlier. Holding both hands out in front of him, he moved his fingers toward his thumbs.

"That's incredible!" Élan's voice was an audible whisper. "The human body is miraculous!"

"Is that what *all* human bodies really look like?" Ashley's light flashed as she spoke. She was fascinated by the silver hair.

"This is what *my* body looks like," Elder Em's gentle green eyes twinkled in anticipation of the next question.

"You mean they're all different?" Jaron asked, his curiosity piqued.

"Quite." He turned with arms outstretched so that all could view his form.

"Well what will *our* bodies look like?" asked Justin.

"Similar to mine," he stopped with arms still open, "except yours will be quite a bit younger. When you're born on Earth you'll start with a baby body suit. Over time it will develop into the suit of a young adult, something like the one you'll wear for the simulation. It's a midtwenties suit, twenty-four or twenty-five Earth years perhaps."

Elder Em snapped his fingers as he spoke, and instantly everyone was transformed. What had initially been a roomful of lights was now filled with twenty-five human bodies.

Élan looked down. His shimmering light was no longer visible. Where the central vortex of his energy had been, now there was a solid mass of chest and torso. He stared at himself aghast; arms and legs had replaced the vibrant extensions of light in his lower aura.

Slowly he turned his hands, lost in the sensation of flesh and bone as he rotated his wrists, turning his open hands upward as he had seen the figures do. Imitating their movements, he touched his thumb to each finger. Then he lost himself in the sensation of squeezing his hand closed, pressing his curled fingers against the fleshy part of his palms.

Finally his hands went up to feel the smooth surface of a forehead. His fingers traced the lines down his brow. Where there had once been sheer awareness, now there were eyes, ears, a nose and mouth.

Looking around he was amazed at the sight of the others. The room was filled with bodies, male and female, large and small. They were all dressed in the same violet suits, yet each body was distinctively different. The color of the skin was different and the body sizes varied. Even more amazing was the variety of hair colors; everything from blond to auburn and dark brown to jet black. At that moment his hands shot up to his head . . .

CHAPTER 2

The Manual

Élan ran his right hand through his short golden blond hair. "What a series of events," he thought. "It was almost too much!" As he raised himself off the bed to release the tension in his hips and torso, a tingling sensation rushed through both legs. Extending his arms above his head to loosen his shoulder muscles, he then bent to touch his toes. He was momentarily astonished by the flexibility of his body.

His head was spinning. So much had changed in such a short time; first there was the revelation of the plan and the presentation of the manual, and then his first sight of Earth, something he would never forget, and now he was wearing a body suit.

Looking around the room, he marveled at the differences in his surroundings. Before wearing a body, he had traveled at the speed of thought and carried his own light, never needing sleep. Now, there were lights and light switches, a bed and a nightstand. The body itself necessitated these changes in the environment. Everything around him served the purpose of supporting its needs.

A few more stretches and he moved to the bed again. Positioning himself on his stomach, he propped the manual on the pillow in front of him. "Even the binding of the book is beautiful," he reflected as he traced the silver letters etched on its cover. The manual definitely carried an energy. His hands tingled every time he touched it. A wave of anticipation washed over him as he opened the cover. To his amazement his earlier thoughts stood out in print before his eyes:

Each and every one of us wants to be the best that we can be!

Had the book read his mind? *To be the best that he could be*, this prayer had been with him forever; a timeless eternity of inner resolve! He thought it was just a simple personal petition, hidden in the secret silence of only his heart. Now to find out that all souls want to do well, all souls want to succeed! Élan was captivated, his curiosity piqued. He read on:

Every soul wants to be a great human being. Every soul sets out with the best of intentions.

But if life on Earth was easy, and all souls were achieving their dreams, this manual would not be necessary.

"How that could be?" Élan was puzzled. He couldn't imagine what kinds of challenges human beings might be facing. "But it must be something," he thought. "After all, the plan was created for a reason!"

Turning the page, he continued with the introduction:

Dear Earth Traveler,

This document is part of a bold new plan for the awakening of mankind and the saving of Planet Earth. Until this time there has not been a written manual containing the goals and guidelines for the planet. As a result, many human beings have lost their way in life.

When a spirit inhabits a physical body a state of amnesia sets in. Many humans have been captivated by Earth's illusions, forgetting that their essence is spirit. In their confusion, many have forgotten who they are and why they were born. Losing sight of the goal they have given up the quest for self-perfection and service to mankind.

There is a purpose to life on Earth. We believe that if human beings are given the proper information regarding this purpose, they will naturally choose to walk the path of wisdom. Herein lies the central theme and intention of this manual and the training that you are about to receive.

Soon you too will be a human being. Our intention is to support you in overcoming the conditions and challenges that you will face as you enter Earth's atmosphere. We have done this by focusing on a set of simple lessons that will support you in your earthly journey.

As you set out on your soul's great adventure, please know that you carry with you the hope of ages in your heart. For the coming span of a short human lifetime, Planet Earth will be your home and classroom. During this time in Earth's laboratory you will have an opportunity for learning and growth in the human experience.

Study well and be happy.

Make the most of your time.

Remember the purpose and the plan.

The Planetary Welcoming Committee

Élan shivered with excitement. His mind was swimming as he raised his head from the book.

"This is it!" he thought, "I'm finally going to have some answers!" It felt as if he'd been waiting for an eternity, but a written manual was more than he'd ever envisioned. He silently thanked God.

Staring mindlessly at a spot on the wall behind the book, he suddenly thought of Zendar. Where was he and how was he doing? Élan wondered if he was looking at his manual.

Zendar . . . Élan sat bolt upright. What if he couldn't recognize his friend? In all the bustle of the morning he'd forgotten to notice what body Zendar had received. What if Zendar was lost, hidden forever in a body suit Élan couldn't recognize? Élan's hand shot up to his face. "What if Zendar doesn't recognize me?" he thought. "It would be awful if we couldn't find each other." His heart raced. What would he do?

Sitting on the edge of the bed, he wondered if wearing a body would change the two of them. Would their interests be different? Would their goals change, and what about their friendship? Élan couldn't bear the thought of losing his friend, especially now that Rhea was gone.

At that very moment, the door to his sleep chamber creaked open. A tall, striking figure with tawny brown hair stood staring at him from the doorway. There was no mistaking the essence of energy. "Zendar, it's you." Relief flooded Élan's body. Their eyes locked.

"I panicked when I realized I didn't know what body suit you were wearing," Zendar said, closing the door behind him.

"Me too!" Élan jumped from the bed and flew across the room to his friend's side.

Suddenly face to face they stopped and the room went into slow motion . . . pulsing to the sound of their hearts . . . hands went up to span the universe of time between them. Their fingers met. It was the first touch of a human hand. They felt one another's energy through their fingertips and knew in their hearts that no matter what physical form they took, they would always be friends. They would always recognize each other. Élan marveled. He'd never felt anything like it.

Moments later it was decided without words; they would study together. Élan chose the window seat. It was his favorite spot in the whole room. Picking up his book, he climbed onto the ledge, positioning himself with his feet against the wall of the enclosure.

Zendar decided on the bed. Lying on his stomach facing the foot of the bed just below the window, he offered to read the text out loud, and Élan agreed.

As Élan shifted in his window seat, preparing to settle in, he caught a wisp of cloud out of the corner of his eye. Something beyond the window always called his attention. He knew it was Rhea. "Where was she now?" he wondered, "and why had she been born so much earlier?" Élan missed her. She would have loved the idea of the training as well as the manual.

Unaware of the sudden change in Élan's mood, Zendar was busy dragging the pillow down to the bottom of the bed with his foot. Fascinated with the dexterity of his new physical form, he propped the book up against the pillow and opened the cover.

Élan was still gazing out of the window thinking of Rhea when Zendar looked up from the text. He studied Élan's face for a moment before he spoke. "It's Rhea isn't it?"

Élan turned his head and nodded. His soft hazel green eyes were distant.

"She really would have loved the manual," said Zendar reflectively.

"I was just thinking the same thing." Élan accepted the continuity of consciousness between them. He was glad to know that wearing a body hadn't changed that. It was something they both trusted and even depended on.

"I wonder where she is?" Zendar's voice was distant. "I'm sorry she's not here for this."

"Me too."

Lost in thought the two of them drifted over the private landscape of their relationship with Rhea. She was an unusually sincere and gentle soul. Her empathy and caring knew no bounds. These were her great gifts, yet sometimes Élan worried about her, for these same qualities often made her vulnerable. The manual would have supported her on her journey.

The three had once vowed never to be separated, and Rhea had promised that if they were, she would try to find them. Élan hadn't doubted it then, and somehow he didn't doubt it now.

"Where will it be, my friend, and when?" he thought to himself. Even though unsure of the timing, Élan knew that Rhea was a woman of her word. The time of her leaving had been so hard. It was the moment when all three were forced to face the truth. They were being sent out alone; each one bound on a separate adventure.

Élan gazed into the mist. His longing for Rhea was

so deep that even now, as he thought of her, he could feel her light. He glanced at his hand gripping the manual and wondered about her body suit. "What did she look like, and how was she really doing?" The thought of her alone out there with no training and no manual left him feeling uneasy.

Zendar shifted on the bed. "Maybe we'll find her." His tone was reassuring. He knew how Élan loved her. He loved Rhea too, but the depth of Élan's longing was almost unfathomable. He seemed to feel things far more deeply than Zendar. His great capacity to love accounted for this extreme sensitivity to the needs of others. Élan was always alert to the feelings of his friends. Zendar appreciated this quality in him. "It'll be OK," he said, silently wishing he could take the pain away.

Maybe changing the subject would help. Turning to the manual, Zendar began to read out loud. It had a soothing effect; the slight strain around Élan's eyes relaxed, and he sat back and began to follow along over Zendar's shoulder.

Soon Élan was lost in thought. Images of the planet floated before his inner eye as Zendar's voice paused to mark the importance of each point as he read.

• • •

PRINCIPLES OF PLANETARY PURPOSE

1. *Planet Earth is a classroom.*
2. *In order to enter Earth's classroom each of you must wear a body suit.*
3. *When you receive your body amnesia will set in and you will forget who you really are.*
4. *Earth's curriculum centers around remembering the spirit and the love that you already are.*
5. *When you do begin to remember the love that you are, your intention to fully manifest that love will be challenged.*
6. *This is because each of you will also receive a Personal Ego and Free Will along with your body when you are born.*
7. *All learning and growth centers around the challenge of rising above the ego to manifest the love that you are.*
8. *Graduation from Earth's classroom depends on fully becoming love in action.*

Élan's heart was pounding as Zendar finished reading the passage. Earth was no longer a distant image. Had he been born already? The book and the bed appeared to be so real, and his body . . . Élan's left hand went up to his face. Which body was this and where was he? Then he noticed Zendar on the bed. No, this wasn't Earth . . . not yet.

Shaking himself, he shifted his weight and swung his legs off the ledge. "Some of the points aren't clear to me," he said as his feet hit the floor.

"Me too, what's 'a personal ego'?"

"That's what I was wondering. Move over, I need to change positions."

Zendar moved against the wall, and Élan rolled onto his stomach and opened his book again. This time they were silent as they reviewed the points for themselves. Still not finding an answer, Élan flipped the pages to the appendix in the back of the book where he read:

• • •

APPENDIX

Every human being is a cell in the great body of mankind, yet because of the amnesia effect and the personal ego almost everyone on Earth has forgotten this. Most human beings look at each other and perceive only the surface differences and not the singular source that lies within.

This is because the ego creates a sense of personal identity that gives the illusion of separation, making me *look different from* you.

Growth and wisdom are synonymous with mov-

ing from a contracted to an expanded state of awareness: from thinking of me *to thinking of* we. *The goal is to expand so that we include all things and all people. Development on Earth is measured by the degree to which we shift our awareness from a small self-centered personal identity to an expanded universal identity.*

Élan pushed himself up. "It sure seems like a bunch of meaningless words to me!" He still couldn't grasp the idea of the ego! It was absolutely foreign to him. After all, there was nothing to compare it to on this side of the window of time. It seemed so strange. "I hope Elder Em can clarify it," he thought as he stood up and walked over to the window.

As the bed shifted, Zendar, whose head had dropped to the pillow moments earlier, rolled over onto his side. "I was dreaming of Earth," he mumbled pulling his legs up to his stomach with his right arm. His head of wavy brown hair was rumpled and his voice had a misty quality as if still in a dream. Zendar was so courageous and strong, yet at the same time there was something so innocent and endearing about him. Élan felt a surge of warmth as he looked down at his friend.

"I saw human beings with beautiful jewel-like lights concealed inside their bodies. No one could see anybody else's light." Zendar was still drifting on the edge between two worlds, touching the border of his dream. "There were many humans wandering all over the Earth on every continent and in every country. They appeared to be lost. Then there was a feeling of emptiness; it was as if I was lost and trying to find my way. Then everything disappeared and I was home again, here on the other side."

"It sounds like the amnesia they were speaking about in the manual," Élan said.

"Hmm," said Zendar. Still curled on his side he watched sleepily as Élan opened the curtain and momentarily peered out.

"It's a strange thing taking a body . . ." Élan's voice trailed off as he gazed into the thick clouds beyond the window. He felt as if he'd entered Zendar's dream. Thoughts of the ego, free will, and separation seemed to collide within him as he stared into the impenetrable fog beyond the window pane.

"And we haven't even been to Earth yet," said a dazed Zendar, his voice hollow.

Élan pulled the curtain closed and turned back from the window, wondering if he'd ever penetrate the mist. Rhea seemed so very far away as he silently sorted through the blend of impressions. There were so many new experiences happening all at once. It was perplexing. "I don't understand," he said turning toward Zendar again. "I've never felt like this before. I sometimes wonder if all these feelings are happening to us *because* we have a body." He faltered in an attempt to clarify his thoughts. "I mean,

I wonder if feeling lost and alone kind of goes with the territory of having a body different from everyone else?"

"Maybe," Zendar said pensively. "We never had them *before* we had a body." He was still in touch with the emptiness in his dream. "I hope we understand a lot more before the next training session begins."

Zendar's eyes shot wide open as he realized what he was saying. The next training session . . . they were going to be late!

CHAPTER 3

The Amnesia Effect

Quickly rounding the corner, Élan and Zendar burst into the course room. They wanted to be early, but in their excitement over the introduction to the manual they had lost track of time. Zendar had left his book back in the sleep chamber. At the last minute he remembered that he needed it for class. This meant making a detour on the way to the training.

There were desks in the class now to accommodate their new bodies, but by the time they arrived only three were left. They were scattered around the room so that Élan and Zendar had to separate. Not wanting to disturb the rest of the students, Élan tried to move quietly through the group, but his breathing was still labored from the run. "Physical bodies are a lot noisier than light bodies," he thought, momentarily overwhelmed with the density in the room. Bodies took up so much space and they carried a different kind of energy. Nothing shimmered any longer and everything seemed heavier.

Still feeling awkward, he moved through the rows toward his seat. A few students looked up as he brushed their desks.

"Patience," he told himself. "Patience and a lot of

practice. I know I'll get better at body-management!" He was determined to be more graceful.

Placing the manual on his desk, Élan tucked himself into his seat, still consciously trying to minimize his movements. Elder Em was talking quietly with Jaron and Brooke in the front row, giving Élan a chance to settle in and observe his surroundings. Turning to view the back wall, he was suddenly aware of a change in the room. Something was different. The atmosphere had shifted from a dignified learning environment to a tone of high adventure. The vacant walls were now covered with posters that alluded to a journey. There was a sense of expectation in the air, but he wasn't sure what it meant.

Completing his conversation with the students, Elder Em moved toward his desk, "How is *everyone* doing?"

"Is that a polite question, or are you really asking?" Justin quipped cryptically.

Elder Em smiled at the question. It went with getting a body. "I was really asking. I'm truly interested in how you're doing."

"Getting used to wearing a body suit is really quite a process, isn't it?" Élan interjected. "I can't speak for anyone else, but I feel a bit clumsy." Most of the students nodded in agreement.

Justin, who had started the dialogue, noticed Ashley out of the corner of his eye as he turned to look at Élan. She looked delicate sitting there listening to the exchange. He wondered why he hadn't noticed her before. "Probably because she wasn't wearing a body," he thought. Wondering momentarily why bodies had such a powerful effect on awareness, he turned his attention back to the teacher.

"Awkwardness can definitely be expected in the beginning stages of wearing a body," Elder Em agreed, referring to Élan's question. "It's the weight isn't it?"

"And the density."

Elder Em smiled, recalling his first experience of physical density. He too had felt totally awkward having to move mass around instead of light energy. "Just give it a little time."

"I can do that."

"Anything else?"

"Yes, there is something else that's really bothering me."

"Even more than the adjustment to the body?" the elder asked. Élan nodded. "What's that?"

"The ego!" Élan's brow furrowed. "What exactly is it and how does it work?"

"That's a pretty tricky subject, Élan." The elder's silver hair glistened in the light. "Earth philosophers have struggled with that very question for years," he mused. "Actually, I'd be interested in hearing your interpretation of it, Élan."

"I think the ego is what makes us feel separate," Élan said reflectively. "I think it's like Zendar's dream."

"You had a dream, Zendar?" The elder turned to

look at the young man, obviously interested. "Tell us about it."

Zendar repeated what he'd seen, describing the hidden jewel-like lights in vivid detail. He finished by sharing the strange negative feelings evoked by the images.

"Quite a dream, Zendar. How do you feel about it now?"

"I felt the emptiness when I awakened from the dream, and I'm still in touch with a strange sense of separation," Zendar reflected. "It felt like a warning, Elder Em. The experience on Earth is really different isn't it?"

"It really is," Elder Em turned to Élan. "And you're right, Élan, the ego is the source of all isolation and loneliness on the planet. However, it's almost impossible to discuss the ego without having a direct experience of it." He began moving through the rows of students as he continued talking. "So we're going to give you a chance to do just that."

"To do just what?" Justin jumped in impulsively.

"Have a direct experience of the ego."

"How?" Justin asked.

"By going to Earth."

"But we're not ready for birth yet." Ashley was perplexed. "I thought there was a training and a plan."

"I'm not talking about birth." Elder Em chuckled to himself. He hadn't meant to scare them. "I am talking about the training and the plan. We're about to begin our first simulation."

"Simulation?" Justin's voice was apprehensive. "What simulation?"

"Remember the three parts to the training: read, meditate, and practice?" Elder Em looked over at Justin as he spoke. "I trust that you've done your reading and meditating so we're ready to begin our first practice session."

The look in Justin's eyes warned him. The amnesia was starting to take effect. "Each practice will come in the form of an Earth simulation." The elder looked around the room as he spoke. Justin wasn't alone. There was now a glimmer of memory loss in the auras of most of the students. "I don't have a choice, the first simulation *must* begin soon," he thought.

"Are you sure we're ready?" Jaron asked, surprised that Elder Em hadn't alluded to this in their conversation before class. With wide-set penetrating black eyes and a slightly olive complexion, one sensed a quiet intensity beneath Jaron's personable exterior. He was an astute listener who was always interested in understanding things. For although inwardly self-reliant, Jaron knew that his confidence rested on preparation and attention to detail.

"You're ready," Elder Em assured. He knew the amnesia wouldn't wait. Once it started, it would only accelerate. "I can see it in your eyes," he added enigmatically.

"We should have known that something was up from the signs on the walls." Ashley's hazel eyes followed the elder anxiously as he moved through the rows of students.

Aware of her uneasiness, the elder stepped directly in front of her desk. She was such a lovely young woman, highly sensitive with an innate depth of insight. He knew she hadn't yet tapped her potential. He was sure that with support she'd be capable of tremendous fortitude.

Drawn to Ashley's presence, Justin leaned forward, watching the momentary interaction closely. The tension relaxed from Ashley's shoulders as she gazed into the stillness in the elder's eyes. "Thank you," she whispered. Elder Em nodded, his energy still holding her as he moved away.

"In the simulation, as in life," he continued, as he moved through the rows again, "you'll be going on a journey. The posters serve as thoughts needed for that journey." He paused, considering whether or not to speak of the amnesia that was now creeping deep into the room. Deciding that they needed to consciously understand what they were experiencing, he continued, "You may notice moments of memory loss or drifting."

Élan's eyes were riveted on the elder. "So that was it!" he thought. His focus kept drifting. He had wanted to be the first to volunteer, but now he grappled with indecision. As his mind attempted to recapture the words in the manual, his memory eluded him. "My mind's definitely wandering," he confirmed out loud.

"What about the rest of you?" asked the elder. A murmur of assent went through the room. "It's the effect of the amnesia that is now permeating the atmosphere. It signals the start of the simulation, so please allow me to give the final instructions before we begin."

His tone was comforting as he continued, "First of all, remember that this is a team experience . . . we are in this together. You will all be able to help each other during the simulation." Elder Em scrutinized the reactions in the room now. "You don't need to worry. If you lose your way or have trouble remembering who you are, the trial and error method of learning will kick in to support you just as it does in real life." This information seemed to have a tranquilizing effect in the room.

Ashley relaxed back into her seat. "You mean if we make a mistake, we'll have a chance to try again?"

"You'll have as many opportunities as you need to learn the lessons, Ashley. Unlearned lessons tend to repeat themselves until they are learned." He turned to face the entire class now. "The simulation, like your Earth experience to come, is based on course correction. Mistakes are really feedback and opportunities for growth. Learn from the feedback and you'll accelerate your rate of development as you progress.

"Now, about the simulations themselves." His hands gestured as he spoke. "We'll be experiencing a total of four simulations. Each module of the simulation will deal with one of Earth's major challenges. When the module is complete we'll bring the volunteer back to the training room so that we can review our progress and do some coaching.

"So," he paused between subjects, "who would like to volunteer for the first leg of the simulation?"

Élan had hoped for more study time. He glanced nervously over at Zendar. "Maybe we could volunteer to go together," he thought. They had discussed the idea earlier, but Zendar was lost in thought now, his gaze distant and remote.

"I'm not sure I understand," Jaron's voice cracked slightly as his confidence faltered momentarily.

"Me either," Justin added, looking over at Jaron, thankful that he wasn't the only one who was confused. "What exactly do we have to do if we volunteer?"

Zendar raised his head in response to the voices in the room, but there was still a faraway look in his eye. For the first time his thoughts were veiled. Élan couldn't reach him. An eerie sensation crept up Élan's spine as he felt the distance between them. "Oh Zendar, not you," he thought, "Don't go unconscious, Zendar!" Just as the thought crossed his mind, Zendar shifted in his seat and looked up. The warm, familiar smile flashed across his face as his eyes caught Élan's stare. With a sigh of relief Élan relaxed into his seat. Zendar winked. He was back, but Élan knew the amnesia was getting serious if Zendar was drifting.

Vowing to maintain his awareness, Élan began counting the fingers on his hands. Slowly and methodically moving his fingers, he became deeply absorbed in counting as the conversation continued around him.

"The aspect of the ego that we will encounter in the first simulation is the aspect of personal endurance," answered Elder Em. "The first volunteer will be discovering the strengthening of will necessary for the ultimate journey."

"What journey?" Justin's mind was hazy and he was having trouble keeping up with the conversation.

Seeing Justin's predicament, Elder Em deliberately slowed his pace. "This amnesia that you're experiencing is the same amnesia experienced on Earth," he said. "Life on Earth is a journey, and the goal is to live from the heart. Yet due to the amnesia men and women everywhere have forgotten this quest as well as the goal." Scanning the energy in the room, Elder Em realized that what he was describing was happening before his very eyes. Students were going through the first throes of deep memory loss, wrestling with the issue of their personal identity and the goal of life. He needed to anchor the lesson before it was too late.

"The metaphor we're using to represent the goal in our simulations is the Cave of Compassion hidden in the heights of Mount Akros. So it is that each volunteer will set out on a journey in search of the cave. However, due to the amnesia, both the goal and the quest will often appear hazy. Some will say that they don't even exist. Thus the will must be strengthened so that each individual can follow his or her inner intuition to finally achieve the objective." With an almost imperceptible gesture the atmosphere rippled open, revealing these words.

Remember the quest; you are on a journey
Remember the goal; to find the Cave of Compassion

"But you were talking about the challenge earlier." Élan looked up as the words dissolved in the air. "Is the amnesia the challenge or is it the fact that many people deny that the cave exists?" He was back in the loop of the conversation. Counting his fingers had kept him focused.

"Both are part of it."

"So what's the rest of it?" Élan was momentarily lucid. "I thought you were talking about something specific that each volunteer would encounter in their portion of the simulation?"

"I was."

"So what's the challenge in the first simulation?"

"Resignation and hopelessness," answered Elder Em. "Many people set out with a goal in life. But when it becomes hazy or adversity sets in, they often succumb. These people let circumstances dictate their lives, never realizing that they have the power to change things."

Listening to the elder's description, Élan faltered for a split second and glanced over at Zendar for support. This time Zendar was with him, his blue eyes held Élan's gaze, filling him with a sense of courage.

"Do the challenges get easier as we progress?" Élan turned back to the elder, hoping for a last out.

"Actually the challenges increase, but so does your capacity to handle them." The elder watched Élan closely as he spoke. "There is a mountain in the simulation that represents the increase in intensity of the quest. Within the mountain lies the goal."

Élan knew he couldn't hesitate. If he didn't go now he wasn't sure he ever would again. This was it. The simulation was about to begin, and he had to decide. His heart raced as he looked over at Zendar again. His gaze was steady, unmovable.

Elder Em turned his attention to the room and said with finality, "Now, we need a volunteer."

"This is it," thought Élan, taking a deep breath. "OK, Elder Em," he said, pushing his chair back and rising from his seat." I'd like to do it. I'd like to go first!"

Zendar watched him proudly. His friend stood tall and elegant as he moved toward the front of the room. "Not too awkward in your body any longer, my friend," he thought as he watched him from the back. "A striking figure," he reflected as he observed Élan's elegant stride. "You'll do well in the simulation! I'm with you," he vowed silently as Élan turned to face the elder for his assignment.

"Good for you, Élan." Elder Em touched Élan's shoulder fondly. "I'm pleased it's you," he said, looking directly into the young man's soft hazel eyes. Élan was momentarily aware of the elder's vibrant energy.

"This is what will happen." The elder turned to the class and raised his voice so everyone could hear. "In a moment I'm going to press the button on the wall's control panel. As I do, Élan will immediately pass through the Window of Time to enter the Earth's atmosphere and the Human Condition. In the same instant, he will immediately forget everything that has happened on this side." He looked at Élan. "Neither the training, nor your friends, nor any of your experiences on this side will be available to your conscious memory."

"You mean I won't even remember you?" Élan asked. He thought of Zendar as he spoke.

"You won't remember anything on this side of the Window of Time," answered the elder. "You'll only remember what you've really studied, for what is committed to heart becomes accessible when we need it." Élan's expression went blank. He wasn't sure what he knew. Elder Em added, "You can depend on your intention, Élan. Our intention will always be realized in the results that we produce."

Élan sighed. "I understand," he said quietly. Although he wasn't sure if his studies with Zendar had been enough, he knew that his intention was strong. He'd have to trust that for now.

Sensitive to Élan's feelings, Elder Em offered gently, "Are you ready to proceed?"

Élan nodded.

"The body suit you're wearing, Élan, isn't the one you'll wear when you're born. But it's perfect for now because it was designed specifically for the simulation. Your clothes, however," said the elder motioning to Élan's violet suit, "definitely won't work on Earth."

Elder Em snapped his fingers, and Élan's clothes were instantly transformed. He was dressed in black jeans, a long-sleeved light blue shirt, and sturdy walking shoes. His feet felt constricted. "This is what they wear on Earth?" he queried.

The Elder nodded. "Trust me! You'll fit in perfectly!"

Élan stared curiously at his wrist. There was a round, flat disk strapped to it.

"That's a watch, Élan. It's for marking Earth time. It's set to begin as soon as you arrive on the planet." Élan's puzzled look spoke for itself, and the elder continued, "The timing we've been using during training hasn't been calculated in direct proportion to theirs. The watch is set according to Earth's time measurements."

Élan nodded. "But . . . there must be hundreds of small differences. How will I ever master them?"

"You don't have to worry about the basics, Élan. Your body will tell you when it's time to sleep and eat. All essential Earth knowledge will be seeded in the mental storage unit of your body suit. You will even know the languages and the basic etiquette of the countries that you enter. In fact, it will seem as if you are well acquainted with the Earth. The goal of the simulation is not aimed at teaching Earth's physical characteristics or man's language and ways. When you're born these things will come naturally during your childhood growth process. The purpose of the simulation is to give you an opportunity to encounter and overcome some of the greatest obstacles that keep people from becoming love in action. Metaphorically, you'll meet challenges and overcome obstacles during your quest to reach the Cave of Compassion."

As the elder looked into Élan's eyes, the tension in Élan's shoulders released. Those eyes carried a peace that Élan had never experienced. "Your love and training will pay off, Elder Em," Élan confided quietly. "I promise!"

"Just do your best, Élan." Touched by Élan's display, he reached over and gently squeezed the young man's arm. "All of us will be with you via transmission, Élan. We'll be experiencing your challenges and your feelings as if they were our own." Turning to the room he added, "As Élan goes through his adventure, we'll participate with him in consciousness. Our minds will be one with his."

Élan's face relaxed, obviously relieved at the news.

Embracing him now, the elder said quietly, "Cherish your mission, Élan, for as you enter Earth's atmosphere the amnesia will intensify. The conditions down there will do everything to counter your intention to achieve the goal."

"You won't let me get lost, will you?" Élan's heart was suddenly in his throat.

"No, Élan, you'll be all right," Elder Em answered encouragingly, and then noticing the apprehension in Élan's face, he added with quiet conviction, "This time I'm the one making the promise." His voice had a stilling effect.

Élan sighed in relief. "Then I'm ready."

Elder Em nodded and reached up for the button on the wall. "Just remember who you are, Élan," he whispered under his breath. As his finger made contact with the button, a crackle and pop of light burst into the room, and Élan's form began to dissolve before their very eyes. Zendar gasped. The spot that Élan had occupied a moment earlier was now empty. His friend was gone.

Chapter 4

The River

The students felt as if they were abruptly catapulted above the landscape, propelled on wings of flight. Instantly, vast horizons with mountains, valleys, and waterways materialized in the vivid three-dimensional transmission just above their heads. An exhilarating sense of excitement and anticipation filled the atmosphere as the vision accelerated and an electrifying gust of wind whipped through the room.

They dipped into valleys, soared above ice-capped mountains, and glided over oceans. Sights streaked by in crystal color, a thousand shades of green and blue, while vivid crests of magenta burst over the horizon and reflected on the desert sand. Time and distance merged in speed. In an instant, vivid day turned to violet night, then back to day again as they experienced the sequence of time on Earth in rapid motion.

Soon forests and fields began to take shape as Élan materialized in the scene high above the earth. He drifted for a while, then slowly floated down and dropped to Earth. Tumbling and rolling, he delighted in the feelings of his body on fresh grass. Lying on his stomach, Élan was mesmerized by the scents of Earth. He'd never smelled anything like it. He rolled over onto his back to view a canopy of blue above his head.

The classroom seemed electrically charged as the seers merged with the scene; Élan's joy was their joy; his feelings their feelings. The aroma of earthy countryside filled their heads.

Suddenly feeling a bit lonely, Élan walked over to an old stump and sat down to consider his predicament. "What a strange and beautiful place this is, but where am I?" he wondered, staring at the landscape around him. "And how did I get here?"

Somewhere in his dim memory, on the borderline of his inner vision, he sensed a huge green-blue orb hanging in space, but he couldn't place the feelings in time. As he pondered his situation, his gaze fell on his hands and arms, and an overwhelming surge of love burst in his heart. Something about the beauty of his body made everything seem all right. "Whatever these feelings are and wherever I am, it's going to be OK," he thought, joyfully turning his attention outward to the scenery in front of him again.

At his feet and as far as his eye could see, tiny yellow flowers dotted the countryside, covering the green rolling hills for miles around. In the far distance, a vast and vivid sea of blue, and way beyond, a mountain jutted upward against a blue sky.

As he gazed at the high mountain, its summit periodically hidden from view by a series of white clouds that drifted above its crest, a subtle feeling like the lilt of a soft song surfaced in his heart. In awe, Élan turned his head in the other direction, and the inner energy immediately diminished. As he turned to face the mountain once more, the gentle sensation began again; it was as if the high mountain was calling him.

Perplexed by the pull, he tested it again and again only to find that it consistently increased or diminished based on the direction of his stance. "The mountain is calling," he thought, finally surrendering to the call that teased at his inner ear and tugged ever so gently in his chest. As he set out in the direction of the mountain, he felt as if he was being gently cajoled. Illusive dreams danced at the edges of his consciousness, heightening his sensitivity.

The sun in the midmorning sky seemed to reflect the joy of the adventure, darting now and then behind fleeting wisps of cloud. The complexion in the course room brightened, filled with the spirit of a quest. Using the mountain as a landmark, Élan cut through patches of trees and climbed the slight hills that dotted the terrain.

As the sun approached its zenith, Élan finally arrived at a dusty road. Hot and sweaty, his shoes soiled from the walk, he turned onto the road, determined to reach the mountain. As he did, those in the room began to relax into the trek with him. The group in the course room started to feel quite confident as Élan strolled over the plains in the transmission.

Suddenly, a strange energy pierced the veil of serenity in the room. Shaken out of their lethargy, the class stared up at the transmission to see Élan approaching the banks of a wide and winding river.

As they watched, Élan knelt at the river's edge, cupping his hands to raise the cool water to his lips. From their vantage point they could see that the massive body of water wound endlessly across the valley floor. He would have to cross it to reach the mountain.

Élan's legs felt leaden as he stared across the water at the mountain looming in the distance. He had already walked for hours. He was exhausted, and the mountain was just too far away! Beads of perspiration glistened on his brow. What made him think he had to go to the mountain anyway? Just because he felt a call, that didn't mean he needed to answer it. It was all an illusion of the mind, anyway. He'd never reach his goal. In fact, there was no goal. Besides, his legs burned from the walk and the mountain seemed no closer than when he'd started early this morning. It was as if it was retreating before him.

"That's it," he thought. "The mountain isn't calling me." He shrugged his shoulders as if to dismiss the thought from his mind. "It's my own craziness

I'm experiencing, probably just an ego trip." He shook his head, determined. "I can do what I want in life, I don't have to go there."

Splashing some water on his face, he ran his wet fingers through his short, straight blond hair, smoothing it back against his head. An acrid mixture of perspiration and water dripped down his cheeks as he stood to view the horizon to his left. Ominous thick gray clouds were gathering in the northern sky. A storm was brewing. "An obvious sign," he thought. "I should turn back."

A gust of wind stirred the trees on the far side of the river as Élan turned to look at the mountain. There it was again: the feeling tugging in his chest, the lightness, the subtle rhythm, like an inner melody. Maybe he shouldn't turn back. Maybe he should keep going. After all, there was something magical in the majesty of the mountain. "There's something about her," he thought. He could feel the pull even though it wasn't clear.

"I've got to try," he muttered finally, and he began winding his way down the thin dirt trail at the river's edge. He moved deftly, his eyes scouring the rocky landscape in search of a narrow spot to make his crossing. Bending now and then to avoid a low-hanging branch, Élan proceeded gingerly, scanning the watery terrain as he made his way down river. Here and there boulders jutted out from the muddy bank, but the river remained wide and forbidding.

As he stepped into a small thicket to avoid a large

protruding rock in his path, a peal of rolling thunder split the air. Climbing a dirt mound to his right, Élan watched as the thick gray clouds began to obscure the sun. To the north the ceiling of sky was already dark. Soon clouds would swallow the final patches of blue above his head. In the distance the heavy rains had begun. A pungent odor filled the atmosphere, announcing the storm's impending arrival.

As Élan turned toward the river, a heavy gust of wind whipped the water into a frenzy of foam. If he was to cross the river, he must do it now.

Looking around, he spotted a large log half-buried on a dirt knoll to his right. "That's it," he thought. "That one will get me across the river." He picked up a sturdy branch nearby and climbed the embankment. Thunder cracked and rumbled overhead as he moved the branch into leveraging position beneath the end of the log. The wind started to wail, tearing at his shirt and flattening his hair against his head. Élan couldn't shake the desolate feeling in his heart. He felt empty and alone, but he had to fight.

Huge drops of rain began pelting down, stinging his face as he used his entire weight on the branch. The log slowly began to move. Brushing the water from his eyes with his sleeve, Élan leaned and pulled on the branch with all his strength. It started to loosen. With a final burst of energy, he reached down and yanked at it. It wobbled, shifted, and finally broke free, rolling down the knoll toward the water.

As if pulled forward by a powerful force, Élan followed the log down the embankment to the river. His heart raced as he stepped into the cold, angry waters at the river's edge. His wet jeans clung heavily, pulling his body down as he struggled to climb onto the log. The wind howled, driving the rain in blinding sheets. Lightning exploded erratically like a deafening giant strobe, sporadically turning the icy river into an eerie, flashing translucence.

Clinging tightly to the log, Élan attempted to propel himself forward by kicking off from a large boulder on the shore. At that moment, the river lashed violently out of control, its liquid claws savagely tearing the wooden beam from his grip. Élan's hand went up in a last attempt to grasp the log as it spun out of reach, and his body was sucked under.

Justin jumped up, as if pulled from his chair. "What are you doing, Elder Em? This isn't a simulation. He's going to drown!"

"Watch," the elder countered.

"While he drowns?"

"Don't be so quick to assume, Justin. Watch . . ."

Thunder exploded in the room, drowning out the elder as the river surged furiously forward, lifting its victim to the surface. For a split second a jagged bolt of lightning illuminated Élan's tormented features as he gulped for air above the waves. His eyes were focused hypnotically on the distant shore. His lips were trying to speak between gasping breaths. The class couldn't hear him above the din of waves and wind, but Zendar who was intently watching his friend, thought he could read the twisted syllables. "Re-mem-ber . . . re-mem-ber . . ."

Then Élan was lost in the wild turbulence as the river lunged, lifting his twisted body and slamming it against a rock that jutted out on the far shore. A stabbing pain seared through Élan's chest as he spun around an angular bend in the river, pulled by the tremendous force of water swelling the banks. "Oh God, where are you now?" Élan's words were eclipsed by a deafening roar of churning water as the eddy at the river's bend turned into an undercurrent, and the weight of his pants pulled him into a downward-spiraling vortex of water.

"Please help me," he cried to an unseen God. Swallowing a mouthful of water as he did, he was dragged under by the swirling current again. Élan felt as if his lungs would burst. In a final frantic attempt, he managed to pull his legs into his chest as he hit bottom. Pushing with the entire force of his body, he propelled himself at a forty-five-degree angle out of the undercurrent and shot out of the water, flailing wildly and gasping for air.

Just a few feet downstream was a large tree growing sideways out of the bank on the far shore. Its branches hung out over a flat rock slab that jutted into the river. Élan lunged forward, grabbing one of the mossy branches. The river raged in raw violence, and his fingers lost their slippery grip. Desperately he reached for the next branch, silently begging for help as he did.

Instantly, a gentle, familiar melody filtered into his semiconscious awareness and his hands found their mark. Clinging tightly to the branch, Élan inched his way toward the bank. The river rushed savagely, pulling at him, and thunder reverberated overhead. Slowly he maneuvered his way forward. Every muscle strained as he finally felt the cold rock surface beneath his belly. With a final heave, Élan wrenched himself forward out of the water onto the smooth stone slab beneath the muddy embankment. The wind whined, turning the rain into a blinding sheet as he groped his way forward. Grabbing one of the tree roots, he pulled himself up and fell into an exhausted heap on the shore.

When he came to, his right hand was frozen, clenched into a contorted fist around the gnarled root. Using his left hand to release his tortured grip, Élan lay on the bank unable to move. His chest ached and every muscle twitched with the strain of battle. Finally looking around, he spotted a large tree farther up the embankment. The sky rumbled overhead and the wind howled, flattening the features on his face as he dragged himself up the slope to its base. Too tired to do anything else, he tucked himself into the base of the tree trunk between its large raised roots, and slipped into a deep sleep.

Zendar loosened his grip on the edge of his desk.

His palms were wet and his heart was racing. Justin looked over at Ashley as he fell back into his seat, weak from his first encounter in the world. He could tell that she was disturbed by the tension in her shoulders, but her thoughts remained concealed behind a reserved exterior.

Jaron looked around the room. Every face was ashen. Brooke leaned heavily back in her seat. Her back ached and her arms were taut with the strain. Moments lapsed before a sigh of relief washed through the room. Élan was sleeping in the transmission above their heads. He had just finished his first challenging day on Earth, and everyone was exhausted.

Chapter 5

Earth's Wounded Heart

Élan grimaced as his cells began to remolecularize in the front of the training room. His head was pounding violently and his shoulders throbbed. "Where am I?" he said, looking blankly at the sea of faces staring back at him.

Zendar stood as if pulled from his seat. "Élan, it's me, Zendar," he said, moving down the aisle toward his friend.

Élan winced, trying to remember what had just happened. Had he been dreaming? He felt empty, dwarfed by the size and intensity of his hallucination. Bewildered, he watched numbly as Zendar came toward him.

As he reached the front of the room, Élan's eyes fell on his own arms. They were scratched and bruised, and his right hand was still curled into a fist. Dazed, he scanned his body. He was still wearing his Earth clothes, tattered and caked with mud from the battle. It hadn't been a dream after all.

Noticing Élan's confusion, Zendar hesitated. "Are you OK?"

"Not really." Élan blanched, straining to comprehend what had happened. "It was awful down there. I kept getting pulled into the resignation and sadness." His eyes stared vacantly at the ground.

Zendar reached for his friend's arm. "What is it, Élan?" He had never seen his friend like this.

Élan looked up at him vacantly. "Something is terribly wrong," he whispered as he slowly began to recognize his friend.

"I don't understand."

"I can't shake the feeling that Earth is in trouble." There was recognition in Élan's pained eyes now.

"How?"

Observing the interaction intently from a spot near the door, Elder Em leaned out of the doorway to check the hall. Justin rounded the corner and entered the class gesturing that he was sorry he was late. Elder Em nodded, closing the door behind him.

Acknowledging Élan's puzzled look, he offered, "We took a short break while you were sleeping in the transmission. Go on, Élan."

Searching the elder's eyes, Élan continued, "I'm just beginning to piece the feelings together," he said, turning back to Zendar as he spoke. His eyes were troubled. "I didn't get it while I was down there. I was too busy fighting for my life in the river."

"That was a metaphor," Justin interjected as he seated himself in an empty chair in the last row.

"I wish I'd known that at the time." Élan's face had a distant, faraway look. "I thought I was drowning."

"I thought so too," Justin added wryly.

"But there's more to it than that, Justin," Élan said. "With all of Earth's beauty, I feel as if something isn't right."

"What makes you say that?" Justin asked.

"The whole time I was down there going through the motions of fighting for my life, I sensed that there was an unspoken message. Something was trying to be communicated beneath the lines of my experience."

"Like what?" Ashley asked from the third row. Her shoulder muscles were still tight from the encounter.

Élan looked up. "I'm not sure, but I know one thing. I wasn't just crossing a river in a storm. There was a message there, even if I couldn't read it." He had the attention of the entire class now, but even Zendar couldn't help him. Élan was the only one who had been to Earth. He sensed the mystery beneath the fabric of human experience. "It had something to do with the intensity of the storm. The elements were angry." Élan stared down at the lacerations on his arms. "It wasn't just a storm," he concluded. "There was a sense of rage beneath it, a sense of being out of control."

"You're right, Élan," Elder Em nodded thoughtfully as he interrupted the dialogue between the students. He hadn't expected such a quick and accurate diagnosis, but he decided to use it. He was pleased with the clarity of Élan's discernment. "Your intuition is accurate, my friend," he said, moving to the front of the room. "Élan's perception is correct." His voice was somber as he turned to address the entire group. "Planet Earth," he said slowly, "with all of its awe-inspiring beauty, is, at this very moment, engaged in a tenuous struggle for life." A hush went through the room.

"So, is that the reason for the training program?" Jaron's dark eyes flashed.

"That's right, and for the sense of urgency you're feeling in our sessions. Why don't you and Zendar take a seat," he said to Élan, pointing to his own seat and another chair against the wall. "I've invited a special guest to join us. He should be able to help us understand these strange feelings that you've sensed."

As Élan and Zendar seated themselves, Elder Em gestured toward the area beside his desk. "Please," he said with a slight nod of his head, "welcome Raoul." A warm wave flooded the atmosphere as he spoke. "Raoul is also a member of Earth's Planetary Welcoming Committee," he added as an imposing figure materialized before them.

Raoul was in a body suit, but he was dressed differently from the rest. A full-length gray robe encompassed his broad shoulders. Gently raising his arms, Raoul removed his hood to reveal a full head of thick brown hair. As he bowed in acknowledgment to the group, Élan lost all awareness of his own pain. Raoul's stature completely captivated him.

The entire group was silent. There was an aura about Raoul, a vibrating field of light surrounded him. His presence filled the room, inspiring a spontaneous surge of love. He was obviously kind, but it was much more. It was compassion one felt in his presence.

"Thank you." Raoul's voice was full with the rich timbre that only wisdom can engender. "Élan is right," he said. "The storm in Élan's simulation was more than a storm." His dark eyes were full with empathy. "It was more than a singular event set against a background of earthly peace and tranquillity. In fact, the storm was symptomatic of a great unrest everywhere. It represented all of the climatic conditions that are raging out of control on the planet right now.

"Let me explain." Raoul's voice, gentle yet firm, carried the weight of complete authority as he moved across the front of the room. Élan was mesmerized. He had never experienced such an energy; stillness at the center of motion that seemed to allude to a tremendous power sustained on the wings of invincible love.

Raoul snapped his fingers and an image of the Earth appeared above their heads. "The people of Earth have lost sight of their true nature. They have forgotten who they are and what it really means to be a human being." A long, jagged fissure appeared at the center of the image just beneath the surface of the oceans as he spoke.

Élan experienced a stabbing sensation as he looked up at the searing lesion that cut through the heart of the planet, discoloring the oceans and continents in its path. A fevered heat burned in his chest and arms, and a jolt ripped through his stomach. It was the same desolate feeling he sensed beneath the surface of his experience on Earth.

"The heart of Planet Earth has been broken by her people," Raoul said. "On every continent Earth's forests are being leveled and stripped. Her ozone layer is being damaged daily and her oceans are being polluted. The balance of Earth's natural food chain hangs on a tenuous thread as entire species are becoming extinct."

A pall went through the room as Raoul continued. "Life without love becomes lifeless. Thus all of the imbalances in nature are a function of man's imbalance. Man's self-serving and self-centered ways have created a reaction. Earth's weather conditions are a reflection of her broken heart. Violent climatic changes and natural catastrophes are escalating on the planet. Volcanic activity is intensifying and earthquakes are increasing. Hurricanes and tornadoes are escalating, and the storm that you saw in the simulation is one of a growing number of flash floods that are inundating areas around the world today."

Raoul began moving slowly through the aisles as he continued. "It is in the hearts of the people of Earth that the breach has been handed down from generation to generation. Neither the trees, the wind, the sea, nor any of the elements of nature carry the breach within them. Like the moon that reflects the light of the sun, nature reflects the energy of man's domination, isolation, and pain," he said, pointing to the heart of the planet as he spoke. "It is man who has created this condition, and it is man who must finally put an end to it on Earth.

"Until now, those who have healed the broken heart within themselves went into hiding or retreat. For until this period of time, the world has not understood nor valued the sweet and the innocent. Those with a purified heart were forced to remain hidden. They had to do their work in secret, away from the eyes of the world." Raoul raised his arms and his tone shifted dramatically as he continued. "However," he said, "the tide on Earth is now beginning to turn."

A note of relief was felt in the room as he continued. "You are about to enter the world at a most opportune time. It is the time of the great awakening. Just beyond the gateway of this moment lies the possibility of the healing of the human heart, the restoration of trust, and the renaissance of wonder on Planet Earth." Raoul paused. "All of nature is awaiting this healing," he added reflectively, "for nature will heal only when human beings begin to heal." Raoul walked toward the front of the room and then turned to face the group again.

"Your mission is to become unconditional love in

action." Raoul's voice dropped. "You see, everyone who heals himself adds to the healing of the whole. Earth will be restored through the healing of its people. It begins and ends with each one of us."

Looking into Raoul's full, dark eyes, Élan felt as if he were standing at the edge of an unfathomable universe. Penetrating yet incredibly gentle, Raoul's eyes tugged at Élan's heart. But Élan was no longer certain. He'd felt the energies on Earth, and this time he wasn't so quick to commit himself. Torn by his own inner turmoil, Élan looked away, unable to hold Raoul's steady gaze. He'd experienced pain as well as joy on the planet, even if only briefly, and he couldn't give himself completely. It hurt too much.

Looking around the room Élan noticed that the sadness was lifting from his friends' faces. Earth's trembling could still be felt, but their individual roles were finally becoming clear. The question of commitment did not seem to overwhelm the rest of the group the way that it overwhelmed him.

Raoul snapped his fingers, and the atmosphere in the room crinkled again. Élan looked up to see the image of Earth slowly beginning to dissolve. It was replaced by a scroll, and as he watched in awe it rolled open in the air above his head. It read:

Your Mission on Earth
Is to Live the Law
of Compassion

As Hundreds
And Even Thousands
Finally Achieve This Goal
the Heart of the Planet
Shall Be Healed Forever

"How can we do that?" Justin's voice broke the silence. "Can one person really make that much of a difference?" Élan smiled to himself; he wasn't the only one who was hesitant.

"One, upon one, upon one." Raoul's answer was rhythmic and repetitive. "Critical mass . . ." Raoul stood still. "The great awakening will occur through all of us. One, by one, by one our individual energies will add up." His voice was resonant. "We can tip the scales of history if each one of us does his or her part."

"But what about the simulations?" Jaron asked. "Are we still on a quest to find the cave?"

"Of course," Raoul answered. "Because the cave represents the place where love resides." He thought for a moment and then added, "In our last simulation we encountered the overcoming of resignation and the strengthening of will necessary for the journey," he said. "In the coming simulations we will discover the mission of becoming unconditional love in action by encountering situations along the way that only love can heal."

Exhausted from his own encounter, Élan glanced apprehensively at Zendar sitting near him at the front wall. Zendar's face seemed frozen, focused forward staring at the floor. His jaw clenched with the intensity of his thought. Suddenly aware of Élan's eyes, Zendar raised his head slightly and winked carefully so as not to be noticed by the rest of the class. Élan was relieved; at least Zendar hadn't wavered. He still needed Zendar's courage. It was a source of strength for him even in a time of personal confusion.

Raoul moved toward Jaron's desk, addressing his dark, quizzical eyes directly. "In our future simulations we will discover the loss of personal power that leads to hopelessness on the planet. We will learn to see the light being buried beneath the personality, molded by parental imprinting and social conditioning. Later, we will discover what happens to people in the absence of strong family ties, when they experience their lives without meaning or purpose. We will then learn how to love without getting love back, finding ways to support the being and not the behavior."

"How are we going to do all this?" Jaron asked. It sounded like a lot to handle.

"Through the study of the nine Matos Mantras embodied in the manual," Raoul answered. "The word *matos* comes from ancient Greece, a culture that reigned centuries earlier on the planet. Matos literally means 'willing' or 'willingness.' "

Raoul slowed down to make his point. "Free will is the greatest gift on Earth. The right use of free will is a central theme in Earth's core curriculum. Therefore, Matos embodies the idea of preparing one's will for a a higher awareness." He crossed his arms and leaned thoughtfully against Elder Em's desk. "The word *mantra* means 'counsel' or 'prayer.' It comes from India, an ancient culture that is still in existence today.

"So the Matos Mantras are prayers of willingness to aid in one's awakening from Earth's amnesia," Raoul said. "They are a powerful set of prayers gathered from a series of ancient manuscripts. Each one of them is specifically designed to assist its user in seeing more clearly the beautiful jewel of spirit that is waiting to be discovered within."

Elder Em, who had been watching the room from his chair in the front corner, stood and walked over to stand beside his peer. "The manuscripts that the mantras came from are part of the ancient glory of past civilizations hidden throughout the world. You see, each of Earth's great teachers carried a part of our message to mankind. Down through the ages the goal of these great beings was to raise the consciousness of mankind. Born into different lands, they delivered the teaching to different groups of people. Students who lived after them inscribed their instructions for awakening on stone tablets or in scrolls, storing them in secret caves and chambers throughout the lands in which they lived.

"Now, in order to enact our new plan for the evolution of consciousness, we have gathered the highest of these teachings from all of the continents," he said. "Through this prebirth training program, your lives will carry the essence of our message for mankind, bringing a multiplication of love that will be felt throughout the world.

"As Raoul said earlier," he continued, "there are nine mantras. Your assignment is to cover the first three for now. Read them and reach within to understand them. Then commit them to your heart in preparation for the next simulation."

"Are there any questions before you begin your assignment?" Raoul asked.

Justin had a few questions, but it felt as if it was the wrong time to ask them. Intuitively sensing that the mantras would tie up some of the loose ends, he decided to hold his questions until after he studied the lessons. He knew he'd have a chance to ask them before the next simulation.

With no answer from the students, Raoul bowed his head slightly to the group. "Elder Em is correct. You are a very special team of people," he said. "I can see why each of you was selected to participate in the plan. I know you'll do well."

The atmosphere sizzled with intensity as Raoul began to dissolve. "Godspeed in your training," he said as he disappeared, leaving Elder Em standing alone at the front of the room.

The elder appeared reflective. Élan noticed that even he felt something in Raoul's presence. Élan shivered. He wished Raoul wouldn't leave. What was this lure, this mysterious attraction he felt in Raoul's presence? Why did he feel so personally befriended, drawn in by his warmth? For a moment Élan regretted his Earth experience. "If only I was innocent again," he thought. Never had he felt such love or such a calling. These feelings were new to him. He'd never been so instantly captivated. "Who are you, Raoul?" he thought, and wondered when their paths would cross again.

CHAPTER 6

Willingness

The sleep chamber was small, barely ten feet by ten feet. Bathed and dressed in his violet suit again, Élan paced, covering the room in three short strides. His hands were clasped tightly behind his back and his head was bowed in deep contemplation. Except for shallow inhalations between thoughts, his breathing was slow, almost nonexistent. Automatically sensing the walled limits of the room, he turned each time he reached the border of his short boundaries. Completely unaware of his surroundings, his mind was powerfully focused.

Images flashed rapidly before his inner eye: his original view of Earth in all its beauty . . . his first sight of human forms pirouetting in air . . . his insight on intention . . . Zendar's dream . . . Earth with its horrifying wound . . . its searing pain within him.

"No way," Élan thought, staring at his hands bearing the lacerations of the planet. He felt the isolation and emptiness . . . the wind wailing around him . . . and the river violently sucking him down. He saw Raoul . . . a powerful vitality born of deep inner serenity . . . Raoul . . . his eyes like deep pools etched in memory . . . his voice, resonant, rhythmic, "one, upon one, upon one . . ."

"Not me," he said out loud. He'd never gone through so many ups and downs in such a short time. The profusion of emotions confused him. "I can't do it, Raoul," he said. A single day on Earth was enough for him. "I can't ever go back there." Stopping in the middle of the room, Élan turned to face the window. His mind was made up. "I'll let Elder Em know tomorrow," he decided emphatically. "I'll catch him before class and let him know I've changed my mind."

Moving deliberately, he drew the curtains back and peered through the pane. He wondered about Rhea somewhere down there. What did she look like? Did she know the emptiness he was experiencing? "Where are you?" he whispered, staring intently into the opaque gray mass in the atmosphere beyond the window. Thick, murky clouds swirled in silent answer to his mind. Dear God how he ached for her. He'd give anything to be able to talk to her just one more time. Did she know Earth's agony? Was she living it now? A wrenching sadness accosted his heart, tearing at the edges of his sanity.

Staring into the fog, Élan lost all consciousness of the room and the window. His breath nearly motionless, thoughts of Rhea consumed him. Stunned by his encounter on Earth, his heart longed for her. If he could only see her, they would talk as they always had, and she would understand as she always did.

Lost in memories, Élan stared into the void. Rhea . . . no distance existed between them, no time. Rhea . . .

As his mind surrendered to his love for her, a whirlpool began to spin in the midst of the condensation. Soon the fog became hazy and wisps of white began to form in the center. As if his intention was penetrating the ethers, a tiny aperture slowly formed in the middle of the clouds. It started as a small light blue hole, finally expanding to about twelve inches in diameter.

Nebulous apparitions began to materialize in the central swirl just beyond his reach. Élan leaned forward, squinting to catch the forms. The shapes eluded him, but the sensations didn't. Somewhere in those misty images was Rhea. He could feel her energy the same way he had felt Zendar's earlier. "Come to me, Rhea." The intensity of his longing consumed him. His chest heaved as if to pull her all the way through the mist. "Come to me," he chanted, pressing his forehead against the window pane. "Come to me, Rhea, just one more time."

Suddenly the door opened loudly behind him. Instantly Élan's concentration wavered and the hole collapsed, leaving a window of white film again. He spun around, his complexion as white as the window behind him.

"Hello . . ." Zendar faltered, seeing the look on Élan's face. "I'm so sorry," he said awkwardly, wishing now that he'd never intruded. "I didn't mean to startle you," he whispered, entering the room slowly. Élan flinched as Zendar placed the manual on the foot of the bed.

"What happened?" Zendar asked as he searched Élan's blanched face for a sign.

"It was Rhea." Élan was staring blankly at the floor trying to recall the feelings.

"Where?"

"Out there," he said, gesturing. "Beyond the window."

"You saw her?"

"No, but I felt her."

"What happened exactly?" Zendar's voice was gentle, apologetic.

"I'm not really sure." Élan's hands were shaking. "It all happened so quickly."

"Start with the course room. What happened after you left class?"

Élan shook his head trying to recall what led up to this moment. He still experienced a dull throbbing sensation when he moved too quickly. "Oh, I remember," he said slowly. "I was disturbed after my visit to Earth. That and the searing wound in the planet left me empty, edgy. I felt lonely and scared. I thought of Rhea and wanted to talk to her just one more time." Élan stood and walked over to the window. "You know, Zen, the way we used to talk."

Zendar smiled recalling the time the three of them had discussed finding each other on Earth. He wondered now if they ever would.

His back to Zendar, Élan gazed out of the window and continued, "I used to stand here and stare out of the window a lot, knowing Rhea was out there, wanting to reach her. But the window was always foggy and dense. It always withheld its secret, until today." He turned back to face Zendar again. "Today a hole opened and hazy images shimmered in the center. And then I felt Rhea's energy. I was mesmerized. It felt as if she was moving toward me. I thought I could almost pull her through." He gestured in acquiescence. "That's when you walked in." Élan turned and sat down on the far end of the bed near the window. Zendar nodded knowingly.

A moment passed. Zendar leaned forward, silently, struggling, sorry that he'd intruded, and at a loss as to what to do. Next time he'd listen to his intuition. Something had told him he should wait, but he'd been so eager to see his friend that his desire overruled his feelings. He vowed never to let that happen again. "Élan," he said finally, deciding that he had to do something, "do you really trust the plan?"

"What do you mean?" Élan was lost.

"I mean do you trust Raoul and Elder Em and the Committee?"

"I guess so. What are you getting at?"

Zendar sat down next to his friend as he spoke. "Do you trust that they know what they're doing?"

"Well, yes." After all, he had before this morning. Élan wondered where Zendar was leading.

"Well, do you trust the plan that they've devised?"

"Sure I do!"

"Do you trust the process?"

"What process?"

"The process of life."

"Come on, Zen, of course I do!"

"Well, if you trust the elders and the plan and the process of life, that covers it all!" Zendar gestured a release with his hands. "Why don't you just let go?"

"Of what?" Élan was confused. "Of Rhea?" he asked, horrified.

"No, not of Rhea. You don't ever have to let go of Rhea, Élan!"

"Of what then?" Élan was totally perplexed.

". . . of trying to control the process."

"Oh that." Élan shrugged and looked down at the floor. "I have."

"What do you mean?"

"I'm not going."

"What do you mean, you're not going?"

"I've decided to resign from the program." Élan was emphatic. "I don't want to be part of the plan."

"Wait a minute." Zendar shook his head trying to understand. "You were just talking about your longing to see Rhea and now you're resigning from the plan?" He threw his hands in the air. "Now *I'm* confused."

"This has nothing to do with Rhea," Élan asserted. "And there is no need for you to be confused. It has to do only with me. This is my mind," he gestured emphatically at his head, "and I've changed it! I don't want to be born."

"What?!" Zendar was flabbergasted. "Wait a minute, Élan, you can't do that! This thing about being a great human being was your idea in the first place. Now you've got me excited about it, and now you're telling me you don't want to go."

"That's right!"

"I don't understand."

"Well if I'd known then what I know now, I would never have committed myself." Élan was insistent. "There's too much to handle down there!"

"So that's it!" Zendar ran his fingers through his hair in frustration.

"That's it!"

"Are you telling me that your answer to a challenge is to quit?!"

"That's right!" Élan's chest heaved in relief. "I just did. It's over. I'm not going!"

Zendar couldn't believe what he was hearing. "One minute you want to be the best human being that you can be, and then, after experiencing your first challenge on the way to the goal, you want to give it all up."

"It was a foolish dream anyway."

"What do you mean 'a foolish dream,' Élan, it's the one dream worth dreaming. You're the one who taught me that. It was you who inspired me."

"Well, I was wrong, Zendar. I had no idea about Earth. I'd never been down there."

"Oh!" Zendar suddenly flashed, sitting back abruptly. "Oh I get it," he said quietly. "This is resignation speaking."

"What do you mean?" Élan turned and looked at Zendar dubiously.

"That's not you. You wouldn't quit." Zendar was certain. "So resignation got you, Élan!"

"That's not true. This is me, Élan, speaking." He tapped his chest. "This is my decision. And I quit!"

"Élan stop." Zendar was aching. He had to reach his friend. "Now you listen to me," he said grabbing Élan's shoulders. "I care about you, Élan, and this voice that I'm hearing isn't yours. It's the voice of resignation. Every word, every phrase reeks with hopelessness. This is what Raoul and Elder Em were talking about. It wasn't just in the simulation. It's here. The simulation was easy compared to this. We have to overcome resignation for ourselves . . . here and now!" He paused. "This is the real test, Élan, not the one in the simulation. *This* is it!"

"What do you mean?" Élan turned to look at Zendar.

"Don't you get it?" Zendar touched his friend's arm. "The simulation was just that, a simulation.

This is the real thing." He grabbed his manual and flipped to the front page. "Look here," he said, pointing to the introductory words in bold print. "Read!" he said.

"I am," Élan answered.

"Out loud!" Élan had never heard such firmness from his friend. He obediently read the text out loud, slowly and deliberately.

Élan looked sheepish as he closed the book. "Resignation is part of the ego, isn't it?" Zendar nodded.

"I thought it was me. I thought it was my decision. I was quitting." Élan sighed. "It was really my ego that was doing the quitting wasn't it?"

"I think so."

"I was even going to give up Rhea. I was ready to give up on the plan, Elder Em, Raoul . . ." Élan shook his head. "I must have been crazy."

Zendar smiled. "Resignation is crazy. It makes us do crazy things!"

"I love her so much," Élan's voice cracked as he slumped back on the bed.

"I know you do, Élan." He paused thinking of the two of them.

"Think we'll ever be together again?"

"Probably."

"What makes you say that?"

"Love has a way."

"I've been really shaken since I've been to Earth," Élan added. "It's hard to know anything for certain any longer."

"It's only hard if you depend on your experience to fuel your faith," Zendar answered. "But if you'll depend on faith alone, your prayers will come from a pure heart." Zendar was reflective. "It's an interesting thing about prayer. Prayers from a pure heart are often answered."

Élan looked over at his friend. What was it about Zendar? He always seemed to have the right words. They always had a stilling effect on him.

"Thanks," he said quietly. "I guess I have a lot to learn." Élan gazed at the floor, thinking of the river. "It was awfully painful down there, Zen. I didn't expect it to be such a challenge."

"It was probably the amnesia," Zendar offered. "We can't discount its effect. I think that's what Elder Em and Raoul were trying to say in their own way."

"I guess!" Élan exhaled sharply. "I sure forgot who I was."

"Right up until this very minute!" Zendar smiled wryly.

Élan eyed his friend as he stood and stretched. "Don't rub it in, Zen." His muscles still ached from his adventure, but it didn't matter now. "Where do we go from here?" he added, hoisting himself up onto the window seat. Still his favorite spot, it was even more of a connection to Rhea now. He curled his legs up onto the ledge.

"How about the manual?"

Élan nodded. "Hand me my book, would you?"

Zendar handed Élan his manual, and they both

began leafing through the pages in search of their place. Zendar found the page first. "Shall I read?"

"Go ahead. I'm ready."

• • •

THE MATOS MANTRAS

Prayers of Willingness for the Awakening of Consciousness on Earth

Remember
(1)

Remember to Remember is a wake-up call for all human beings living on Earth. Remember to Remember who you are means remember that you are spirit living in a physical body. Remember to Remember why you're here means remember that the goal on Earth is unconditional love.

You are spirit inhabiting matter. The body is a shell, an outer encasement, a vehicle in which to live while on Earth. Train your sight to look within; focus on the source beneath the surface. Continually refocus your attention on the root and not the stem, and you will finally condition your mind to go beyond physical appearances.

Listen
(2)

Listen! There is a song for every soul that plays like a fountain at the heart of every life. Listen to your own life song. Be ever sensitive to her calling. When you are caught in the storms of life, her sweet silver sound will lead you home. Her resonant internal tone will keep you attuned to truth and help you correct your course along your way.

Follow your own life song. Seek her counsel, and she shall guide you. Renew yourself in her inner stream, and she shall inspire, instruct, and uplift you. Open your heart to your own pure song, for she shall carry you through to the goal and the fulfillment of your destiny.

Ask
(3)

Ask for help. Ask for solutions. Ask for guidance. Ask for insights. Ask for support. Ask for your needs to be fulfilled.

Because of the Free Will Factor, the One waits in the wings on the stage of life until invited in. By asking, you open the door so that the One can assist you in your life journey.

Asking is one half of the mantra, the other half is being willing to receive. Listen and be ever alert, for when the universe answers, it may be in the language of little synchronicities that guide you toward a solution. Ask knowing that an answer is forthcoming. Then be ever alert to catch it.

Élan was incredulous. The mantras had encapsulated his entire Earth experience. As he closed the book, he silently prayed that he'd never forget who he was again.

CHAPTER 7

Broken Dreams

Elder Em was standing unobtrusively against the wall behind his desk as the students arrived. He watched closely as Élan and Zendar entered the room, manuals in hand. This time the two were early. Centered and inwardly reflective, they were somehow different. Zendar gestured to a couple of empty seats in the third row, and Élan quietly seated himself beside his friend.

The elder noticed that he seemed especially introspective. Élan had always carried a special light, a special enthusiasm, but now that enthusiasm was softened by an aura of humility. His zest had been tempered by experience. A sense of inner composure permeated the atmosphere around him. It was a quality that hadn't been there before.

The elder had been concerned at the close of the last session. The simulation had been far more effective than he had hoped, and Élan had been physically and emotionally drained when he left the training room. "The integration time has been good for him," Elder Em conjectured, secretly relieved. Élan wasn't fully aware of his importance to the plan yet, but the elder knew that this young soul would need both his inner assuredness as well as his new found poise to accomplish his task on Earth.

And then there was Zendar, always forthright but with a new sense of purpose in his stride now. He appeared to be more self-possessed. Élan's adventure had deepened his inner resolve. "The Committee will be pleased," he thought, noting the change in both of his students.

He knew, however, that they were still in the early stages of preparation. "The real proof is yet to come," he thought. He realized that both of these souls as well as all the others still had a long journey ahead of them. Their success in the training would only be measured in each of their lifetimes ahead. "They will all have to pass the test of life on Earth," he nodded to himself. There was a lot of work yet to be done.

"Welcome back," he said, stepping out from behind his desk. "How are you doing?"

"Well, I'm back," Élan answered flatly.

"We're glad to see that, Élan."

"It was debatable, you know."

"How's that?" the elder asked, realizing that his apprehensions had been accurate.

"It was harrowing!" Élan paused. "I had to go through recovery after my first Earth experience," he said, gesturing in Zendar's direction as he continued. "If it hadn't been for Zendar, I'm not sure I would have made it."

"So when you say you're back, does that mean you're ready to volunteer again?" the elder quipped.

"I think I'll sit this one out," Élan laughed, feigning generosity. "I'll let someone else have an opportunity to grow from their experience, thank you."

"What's the second challenge?" Justin cut in. He was curious. Fascinated by Élan's adventure, he wondered how he would do down there.

"The second challenge is the Challenge of Broken Dreams," Elder Em answered.

Jaron was also listening attentively to the exchange from his back-row seat, wondering how he'd do on Earth. Normally confident, he had been shaken by Élan's encounter. Back in his sleep chamber, self-doubt and misgivings had flooded him. Finally, in an attempt to regain his composure, he had turned to the manual, memorizing each mantra and practicing them out loud. He'd even gone over to study with Brooke. In the final time before class the two of them had engaged in a rigorous dialogue regarding Élan's adventure in relationship to the mantras. Engrossed in the elder's conversation now, he wondered about his own chances for success if he volunteered. "I'm not sure I understand," he burst in spontaneously. "What about broken dreams?"

"Broken dreams are a big issue on the planet." Elder Em turned to look at Jaron as he spoke. "Everyone on Earth has experienced hopes and dreams that don't come true, Jaron," he said. "The question is, how do we deal with broken dreams? How do we learn to go on in spite of setbacks?"

Recoiling at his own sudden outburst, Jaron looked over at Brooke. She knew his hopes and dreams as well as his uncertainty, and she believed in him. Their time together before class had confirmed her intuitions about him. Jaron was incredibly capable, but he needed to take that first step to get beyond his apprehension. Holding his gaze, she encouraged him with an almost imperceptible nod of her light brown head.

Jaron momentarily shuddered with the awesome responsibility he felt for the task ahead, then abruptly turned back to the elder, determined not to falter. "I'll go," he said loudly, stunned at his own forthrightness. He cleared his throat self-consciously. He hadn't meant to be so abrupt, but he was afraid he'd change his mind. "I'd like to do the next simulation, sir," he said, standing quickly so as to bypass his considerations.

"Great Jaron," Elder Em answered, gesturing him to the front of the room.

Brooke smiled as her friend walked to the head of the class. She knew his sensitivity, but she also knew his strength. She sensed his abilities even more than he did, and she silently wished him well as he joined the elder and turned to face the group.

"Every simulation rests on the shoulders of the last one." Elder Em reached out and touched Jaron's shoulder. "You'll arrive on Earth a short distance beyond the river that Élan crossed. Our learning is cumulative and the goal is the same in all of the simulations." Jaron looked down at his violet outfit questioningly as he spoke. "Of course," he added, stepping back from his student, "your new clothes."

Élan smiled to himself, remembering his own apprehensions in the front of the room. Jaron was now dressed in Earth clothes: light blue twill pants and a white short-sleeved cotton shirt. On his left wrist was the familiar circular disk that marked Earth time. Élan rubbed his arm thoughtfully as he viewed the scene from his third-row seat.

"Any questions?"

"Not right now." Jaron glanced at Brooke, who gestured slightly indicating her support. "I'll probably have a few when I'm down there," he said looking into the elder's eyes.

"Are you ready then?" Elder Em held his gaze.

"As ready as I'll ever be," Jaron nodded, still a bit hesitant but intent on getting on with it. He'd wanted to go, and with Brooke's encouragement his confidence had returned.

"Just do your best and trust the process." Elder Em moved toward the front panel as he spoke. "It's morning on Earth. Have a great day." With that the elder hit the button and the atmosphere crackled with electricity.

The class looked on as Jaron began a slow dissolve in a luminous lavender swirl. Morning was breaking as the scene burst into view. The indigo spell of night cracked in a silver sliver along the horizon line just beyond the mountain. Iridescent rays of orange and pink spilled out of the crack to cover the land as Jaron appeared on the screen, a solitary figure standing on a hill in a large field of yellow flowers dappled coral in the morning light. Dawn filled Jaron's senses. He'd never experienced so many sensations at once: colors washing across a field of tiny flowers, the crisp, clean smell of dew, and the sound of birds chirping as they greeted the day.

Looking around, Jaron was suddenly overwhelmed by a poignant sense of personal solitude. There was no other human being in sight, only rolling fields and a vast winding river in the distance below him. It appeared that he had climbed the hill on which he was standing and that he was headed in the direction of a high mountain outlined in the distance before him.

Struggling to remember where he was and why, Jaron finally walked over to a tree at the edge of the field and sat down on a large sprawling root to contemplate his situation. From his vantage point he could see portions of the river winding across the flat land to his left beneath him. To his right was the mountain, a towering peak rising in the eastern sky. As he gazed in the direction of the mountain, Jaron felt an energy in his chest, a compelling sense of urgency pulling him forward. "That's it," he thought, standing abruptly. "Even if I'm not sure where I came from, that's where I'm going." Finding a branch under the tree, Jaron stripped the dead leaves from its bark, fashioning a walking stick as he began a brisk stride in the direction of the mountain.

Soon his surroundings captured his attention. Fascinated with every new discovery, Jaron's pace slowed. Flight seemed a miracle as he observed birds passing overhead. The wind that rustled in the trees and brushed against his skin delighted his senses.

In this way, he continued on his walk toward the mountain. Hills and valleys rose and fell beneath his feet as the sun continued its trip across the daytime sky.

High noon burned down on his brow as he finally reached the top of what had been a distant hill earlier that day. Below him, stretching as far as the eye could see, was a clear blue sea. To the left and at a distance along the shoreline was a village built on the slope leading down to the edge of the sea. Here and there islands dotted the surface of the water, and in the distance beyond loomed the mountain. Its majestic silver crest carved a spectacular line high above the edge of the far horizon.

Spotting a dead tree trunk lying on the hillside, Jaron walked over to it and sat down to rest. Enthralled with nature, he'd lost all awareness of bodily sensations, but, as he seated himself, physical impressions flooded his consciousness. His throat was parched and the muscles in his legs ached from the walk. Laying his walking stick against the trunk, he kicked off his shoes and began to massage his blistered feet as he gazed down at the sea. The sun was dancing on the water's surface, turning it into a shimmering pool of sparkling silver azure and emerald crystals.

Rubbing his tender feet, Jaron stared down at the sea wondering how he'd ever cross it to get to the mountain in the distance beyond. He knew he had to go there, but he wasn't sure how to do that. Scanning the shoreline to the right, his eyes finally fell on a solitary figure working at the edge of the water. He seemed to be cleaning a cylindrical container of some sort, scrubbing something from its sides.

Still hot and tired, Jaron picked up his stick and began a slow descent to the sea. His legs burned as he headed in the direction of the figure on the shore. As he approached he could see that a man was scraping barnacles off an old wooden boat. A small motor lay on a tarp a few feet away. It had obviously just been scrubbed. The man stood and turned to greet him.

"Hello there," he said. He was wearing an old straw hat with a wide brim that shaded his weathered face and neck from the afternoon sun. "The name is James," he added, extending a wrinkled hand toward the young man.

"The name's Jaron," he said, duplicating the man's gestures.

"Been walking a long way?"

"Quite a distance."

"How 'bout some water?" he asked, pointing to Jaron's right where a large brown jug stood on an old tree stump.

"Thanks," Jaron said. Resting his stick against the base of the trunk he raised the jug to his mouth and took a long swig.

"What are you doing out here by yourself?" asked the old man, tipping his hat back to examine Jaron's perspiration-stained face. His slightly olive complexion was darkened from the sun. His shoes were covered with dust and his shirt was soiled with sweat. He'd obviously been walking a long distance.

"I'm on my way to the high mountain." Jaron wiped the water from his mouth as he replaced the jug. "And I need to get across the sea."

"Hmm," said the old man, as he rubbed his unshaven chin with hands coarse and leathery from years at sea. He was scrutinizing the young man carefully. He wasn't prepared for climbing, so what was the real story? "What brings you to these parts?"

"Just traveling through."

Suspicion shadowed the seaman's complexion as he continued. "What makes you think that you can cross that sea, Jaron?"

Jaron felt uneasy at the tone of the old man's question. He had expected encouragement, even help, but there was something forbidding in the old man's gestures.

"I don't know," he answered. Having made an instant decision not to be too candid, he reached for his walking stick. "Just like the looks of the mountain, I guess." Jaron glanced at the mountain, pretending nonchalance. "Anyway, I thought I'd go and see it. After all, I like to climb."

"Hmm!" James shrugged, muttering under his breath.

"Did you say something?" Leaning on his walking stick, Jaron raised his right hand to shade his eyes as he looked at the old man.

"Not really," the old man answered impatiently.

"You said something, James" Jaron insisted. "What was it?"

"I said you might want to reconsider," he said gruffly.

"Why would I want to reconsider? That's a beautiful mountain and I'm out for an adventure."

"You'll have an adventure all right," he answered, irritated with Jaron's insistence.

"What do you mean?"

"That's no ordinary mountain, son," he said, shaking his hand in the direction of the mountain. "Her name is Akros, Mount Akros." He eyed the mountain respectfully as he spoke. "Akros means 'topmost.' She's the highest mountain in the whole area, and many say she's the most dangerous." His voice was flat. "At a distance Akros stirs wonder in the soul, son. Many people have begun their journey bound to reach the high country." He nodded in the direction of the mountain as he spoke.

"But as you get nearer to her, you'll find her to be deadly. Her cliffs and peaks are among the sharpest and most treacherous in the world. Many a seasoned climber has been known to turn back upon reaching her base." He paused, and then added emphatically, "That is, if they even get as far as her base."

Adjusting his hat, he continued. "No, son, the mountain isn't for you. Wanting to climb her is a dream, just a young man's folly!" He paused, looking long at Jaron as if to measure his intent. "You'll give up like the rest of them!" he mumbled, turning back to work on his boat.

"Not me, James, I'm not like the rest of them. I have to go there!"

"If it's just a beautiful mountain, why is it so important to you?" The old man looked up from his work, eyeing the youth skeptically. "I can show you some other beautiful mountains. You can climb them."

"Thanks, James, I'll probably take you up on that offer sometime," Jaron answered lightly. "I don't know why, but I think I'd like to give that one a try for now."

"We'll see," answered the old man as he turned back to his work. "I've heard many a person say they were going to give Akros a try, but when the time came, they all turned back in fear." His tone was conclusive, letting Jaron know that he intended to go no further with the conversation.

Jaron was momentarily lost, unable to understand

why he was having such a hard time reaching James. Intuitively he softened his approach. "I guess you're right, James. After all, few have ever reached Akros and fewer still have scaled her peaks successfully." Jaron shrugged. Walking over to the tree stump, he seated himself next to the jug. "Why should I be any different?"

"Now you're talking." The old man winced in the glaring sun. "You're smart to leave the mountain alone and get on with your life."

Jaron stared down at the ground reflectively. "How come life is so uncertain, James?"

"What do you mean?" The old man turned toward Jaron inquisitively.

"I felt as if the mountain was calling me." Jaron gazed wistfully at the mountain as he spoke. "But you're telling me that lots of people feel that way."

"That's right."

"And they all turned back?"

"U-huh," James nodded.

"Am I really that different, James?"

"What do you mean?"

"Am I the only one who wants to go after it?"

"Go after what?"

"My dream."

"I'm not sure I understand." The question caught the old man off guard.

"Didn't you ever have a dream, James?" The old man looked up at Jaron, still seated on the stump staring up at the mountain. "Didn't you ever stop to think that there must be more to life than meets the eye, a deeper significance than all this? And didn't you ever long for something better?" His tone was so disarmingly gentle that it slipped through the earlier facade and struck the very taproot of James's experience.

The old man gazed into the young one's deep brown eyes and lapsed into silence. He nodded reflectively, remembering another time. He was younger then, and there were dreams. "Of course I've had my share of dreams," he said. "Everyone does." A distant vision floated across the old man's face.

"I loved the quest," he said, smiling at the memory. His face looked suddenly younger as he gazed off in the distance."Like you, Jaron, I believed I could do anything, accomplish any goal, achieve whatever I desired." A light shone in the old man's eyes now. "I was strong in those days, courageous and bold, willing to take on the world." He smiled and straightened his shoulders. "Life was really different in those days," he sighed.

"It was then that I heard of Akros and the cave. There was mystery there and, like you, I vowed to find it for myself." The old man suddenly recoiled, as if having seared his fingers on a flame that burned too brightly. "But I was younger then," he said, shaking himself as if to throw off the web of memory. "I didn't know any better."

He turned sharply back to his boat. "Now I just

keep my mind on my work," he said gruffly. "I fish these waters, but I know better than to attempt a crossing anymore."

Jaron shuddered. The cave! He hadn't heard a word after that. The words sent a chill through his whole body. "What cave?" he asked, jumping from the stump.

"None of your business, son. It's best you just forget we ever had this conversation," he said. Lifting his knife, he turned abruptly to finish his job.

"But what happened, James?"

"What do you mean, what happened?"

"Why did you give up?"

"I didn't give up. I got the message," he answered sternly without looking up.

"What do you mean you got the message?" Jaron was insistent. "Didn't you even try to get to the cave?"

"Of course I did."

"Well?"

"Well, what?"

"Well, what happened?"

"Well," he sighed slowly, turning in Jaron's direction again. "What happened?" He raised an eyebrow thoughtfully. "That was such a long time ago, Jaron." He shrugged and shook his head. "Can't we just drop it?"

"Please." Jaron's eyes were wide with pleading. What was it about him? James had never had a conversation with a stranger like this. Maybe it was because the young man felt so familiar, a part of his own youth that had slipped away. He felt as if he understood his longing.

"Well, I put a lot of thought into it," he answered slowly. "I planned my journey thoroughly, right down to the dried meats to be rationed for the climb." He smiled, momentarily recalling the days of preparation. His mother had been alive then. She had helped him, all the while shaking her head and warning of the dangers of young dreams. He thought it was just her age. He hadn't listened to her then.

"And?" Jaron pressed.

"And . . . I set out to cross the sea." He could still see his mother standing at the seashore that day. She was wearing a light blue apron, waving, a worried look still on her face but trying to be brave.

"What happened?" Jaron wouldn't let go.

He shook his head. "A few hours out, the sea raged and broke against my boat, shattering it into a hundred pieces. They found me semiconscious on the shore and pulled me out." He turned back, reaching for his nets on the far side of the boat. "She didn't say anything after that," he mumbled as if to himself. "She didn't need to. The message was loud and clear."

"What did you say?" Jaron couldn't make out the words.

"The message was loud and clear," he said over his shoulder.

"But what about the cave?"

"What about it?" he said gruffly.

"Tell me about the cave!"

"What do you mean tell you about the cave?" The old man was pulling harshly on his nets now. "Don't you get it? The cave isn't real. The cave is a phantom hope, a mirage to a thirsty soul."

"What's the name of it?" Something was driving Jaron, a feeling, an urgency. He didn't know what it was.

"It's the Cave of Compassion, but never you mind, boy. If you haven't heard about the cave before, it's best you don't hear about it now. Life was better when I didn't know about her." His tone was curt.

"The Cave of Compassion?" Jaron hadn't heard the rest of it. The name sent a shiver down his spine. "Is the cave somewhere on Akros?"

The old man stood back from the boat, studying Jaron closely now. "Some still believe so, son, but others have always called it a silly rumor." He shrugged his shoulders. "I think they're right. Give it up, son." He pushed his hat back as he spoke.

"I can't." Jaron's face was imploring. "Please won't you help me. Just help me get across the sea, please."

"I told you, it can't be done." He wished Jaron would just give up like the rest of them. Why did he have to be so obstinate? "I've already tried," he said finally.

"But only once," Jaron countered, "And not with me."

The old man couldn't help but smile. This kid was as stubborn as he had once been. "What difference does that make?"

"Sometimes it takes two or three times to get the hang of it."

"You're really persistent aren't you?" The old man stared into Jaron's wide-set, dark eyes. He liked him in spite of himself. Something about the young man was endearing. For a moment he felt as if he was looking at his own reflection many years ago. He liked himself then. How he wished there had been someone to help him back in those days.

"You never know, James, with our combined energies things might work out this time!" Jaron could feel him softening.

"Well, I don't know," he said. "It didn't work the first time." Reaching into his pocket he pulled out a soiled handkerchief and began rubbing the beads of perspiration off the back of his neck.

"But things were different then." Jaron pleaded, "Please give it one more try."

"Well, maybe."

"Just across the sea, James, please." Jaron sensed just how far he could push now. "No further, I swear."

"Well, I can't take you all the way across the water. I can only take you as far as I have gone myself, and I've never gone all the way to the shore on the far side of the sea." His voice was reflective. "But I have gone as far as those islands," he said, pointing to the outcropping in the middle of the vast body of water. "So, if it'll help you, I could take you that far. I guess I could do that much for you," he conceded.

"Oh thank you, James." Jaron couldn't hide his elation.

"Come on." The old man was smiling openly as he turned toward the weatherworn boat.

"How come you're smiling, James?"

"Oh nothing. Just a private thought."

"What is it?"

"I just thought of my mother." He gestured in the direction of the boat as he spoke. "Help me get the motor on this thing and we'll launch it."

"What about your mother?" Jaron walked over to the motor with him as he spoke.

"I sometimes wonder if she hadn't secretly wanted me to win."

"What do you mean?" Jaron asked, bending to lift the engine.

"Well she was there the day I left, and even though she had admonished me not to go, I sometimes wonder if she was disappointed when I didn't make it."

"She never talked to you about it?"

"Never said a word." James wondered about the cycle of life as they silently carried the motor down to the shore. His son and grandson still lived at home with him. His son had tried to leave once, took his two-year-old with him, went away and took a job. James had wanted so badly for his son to make it, but something happened and he returned within a few years. "He never said a word," he thought. Even when James had asked him, he refused to talk about it.

"But I wonder," James said, finally breaking the silence as they eased the motor into the back of the boat, "doesn't every human being long to follow their dreams?" He saw his young grandson's eyes as he spoke. Maybe there was still hope.

Jaron stopped and looked into the old man's eyes. There was a light in them again. Jaron had reached him for a moment. "I think so, James," he said quietly. "But it's the commitment to pursue our dreams that counts. Most people give up at the slightest obstacle."

"Like I did?"

Surprised by his candor, Jaron nodded gently. "You probably just didn't understand the process."

"I guess it kind of hurt my pride, being found semiconscious like that." James grimaced slightly at the thought of all the neighbors finding him on the shore that day. "Unconsciously I think I was expecting an immediate result," he said. Then he added thoughtfully, "It doesn't happen that way does it?"

"Not usually." Jaron was reflective. "Usually there's lots of small failures on the way to the goal.

The secret is to learn from them so that you get better as you go."

James nodded. "But my failure was a big one."

"Big or small, a failure still provides feedback. If you want something bad enough, you've got to keep going."

The two worked silently for a time. Lifting the motor between them, they maneuvered it into position. James showed the young man how to secure it in place by locking down the side latches. The boat was about ten feet long and easy to manipulate. Together they hoisted it into the shallow waters at the edge of the sea. Holding the boat tightly with both hands, the old man gestured toward the stern with a nod of his head. "Jump in and I'll push off," he instructed.

Relieved at the shift in energy and thankful for the help, Jaron walked into the water up to his knees. Grabbing the boat, he pulled himself up with his arms and lifted one leg over the side. By heaving his weight forward into the hull, he was able to drag the rest of his body up and over the side landing somewhat clumsily on the floor.

Used to entering the boat after pushoff, the fisherman followed, gracefully easing himself over the rim. Both of them were wet nearly to the thighs as they got the motor started and headed out to sea in the direction of the islands.

The sea was calm at first, and they rode quietly

without a word. James was seated in the stern, his hand on the steering stick. Jaron sat in the prow of the boat, his dark brown hair lifting in the wind.

As soon as they were beyond the quarter-mile mark in the water, the sky began to change. Large, gray cumulous clouds formed on the horizon just beyond the islands. Soon the climate in the boat shifted. Jaron looked back at the old man. The light was gone from his eyes and his skin was ashen. Thunder ripped across the sky from end to end, and the old man's face was frozen with fear remembering another time. Jaron tried to shake the feeling in the old man's eyes. It was déjà vu. Where had he felt these sensations before—the thunder, the sense of isolation and loneliness, the worthlessness of the attempt? The clouds were gathering speed, rolling toward them.

Self-doubt instantly flooded Jaron. He felt as if he was drowning; the sadness consumed him. "The old man was right," he thought. "This is reality. The dream was futile. The islands look so far away."

Gazing up at the gathering storm in the sky, Jaron finally succumbed to the sensation of being sucked down. "It's worthless to attempt the trip." He felt as if his breath was being crushed violently from his chest. "Why not give it up?" he thought. "Obviously those who came before me were right."

The old man broke the silence. "I knew we shouldn't have come."

"What did you say, old man?" Jaron winced as another jolt of thunder split the sky.

"I said that I was a fool to listen to you," shouted James over the roar.

"I can't hear you." Jaron shook his head, trying to hear him above the slap of waves rising on the sides of the boat.

"I said, it's no use." he shouted above the din.

Jaron tried to read the old man's lips, repeating the words slowly in an attempt to pierce a hole through the fog of melancholy.

"I'll take you home now, son. You're making the right decision." The seaman moved to turn the boat around.

"Wait," Jaron said. The motion had sliced through the haze, and Jaron bolted toward the old man. "We've got to fight it."

"It's no use."

"But you promised."

"Promised what?" The old man was impatient now. The storm was growing in ferocity. This boy was a fool!

"To take me to the islands."

"Can't you see it's useless?"

"Just keep your promise," Jaron's voice was firm as he began to penetrate his own confusion.

"Let go of your childish dreams. Most people have come to their senses by your age."

Instinctively Jaron knew that he needed to connect

inwardly. Turning his attention to the One, he silenced his mind.

A resonant voice reverberated on the periphery of his awareness: "*Remember to Remember.*"

"Remember to Remember *what*?" Jaron silently held the question before his mind's eye. Moments passed. "Remember who you are. Remember why you're here."

A wind whined sharply across the water, startling Jaron out of his momentary stillness. Waves turned to sharp white foam lashing against the small vessel. The old man clutched the side of the boat as it pitched back and forth. "I knew it," he screamed above the waves. "We should never have set out on this journey. The gods are angry!"

"Stop, old man, it's not true." Jaron was clinging to the wooden seat in the center of the hull, but the pounding waves ripped his hands from the post and threw him to the floor of the boat.

Jaron was suddenly lucid. "The gods support our intention, but your intention is not aligned. It's split, pulled in two by your own inner fears. When we waver, the world wavers with us."

"What do you mean?" James moaned. Caught once more in the web of prolonged amnesia, the conversation slipped beyond his reach now.

"Remember to remember who you are, old man," screamed Jaron, in a last attempt to reach James's being.

"Even though the climate on Earth overtakes us,

we are human beings, and we must fight back. As human beings we're bigger than our circumstances and far bigger than our emotions, bigger than the sadness or despair that sometimes laps at the edges of our minds." As Jaron's voice subsided, a muted tune began to dance in the distance above the waves, and the sea instantly turned crystal calm once more.

It was a rhythm, an energy he'd sensed before. As it approached, Jaron could distinguish a melody. It called at the center of his being. His heart opened to its pure soft rhythm, and strength began to flow into his limbs. Soon a vigorous energy filled his chest and his mind cleared. He felt instantly calm, detached from his surroundings. His inner world had triumphed over the outer illusion once more.

James was still sitting in the stern of the boat clinging to the rudder. His face was ashen, but his eyes were curious. Stunned by the rapid chain of events, he peered up at the sky. It was clear, and the waters were calm as far as the eye could see. It had all happened too quickly: first the storm and the raging sea, and his sense of hopelessness, and then the sudden shift. He'd heard of men with mystical powers. He stared dubiously at Jaron. Was he one of them? Where did this young man really come from? And why was he here?

"Who are you?" he asked furtively.

"What do you mean who am I?" Jaron shot a quizzical look at the old man huddled at the back of the boat. "I told you, I'm Jaron. Look," he added pointing to the island, "the main island is in clear view now."

James blinked nervously, following Jaron's direction. A long white beach stretched the length of the side of the island closest to them. It was only a mile or so away to their left.

"What just happened?"

"If you want something bad enough, you have to choose and rechoose every step of the way, James." Jaron moved back to where he was seated as he spoke. "Let's restart the motor, and you can drop me off at my destination." He smiled at the old man who was still in a state of shock trying to integrate his experience. "You'll be home in time for dinner," he added, reaching for the choke.

After a few attempts the motor sputtered and coughed to a start, and James headed the boat in the direction of the beach. Jaron heard him muttering something under his breath as he seated himself in the helm. The rest of the trip was smooth. The afternoon sun cast a wavery shadow at the bow of the boat as they pulled into the shallow turquoise waters surrounding the island. Carefully maneuvering between the coral and rocks just beneath the surface of the water, James pulled the boat into the shallows.

"This is it," he said cutting the motor. "You'll have to get a bit wet, but it's late afternoon. There's still a few hours before sundown. You'll dry off by then."

"Thanks, James, I really appreciate the support."

Jaron was still. The only sound was a gentle lapping of water against the sides of the boat. Looking directly in James's eyes, he reached out to shake hands with the old man as he spoke.

"But what really happened out there?" James was still uncertain.

"What do you think?" Jaron's question was rhetorical.

"I'm not sure."

"Not every thing is as it appears to be, James."

"I think maybe I should have tried again, those many years ago." James had a wistful faraway look in his eyes. He thought of his young grandson again. Maybe it wasn't too late to break the cycle. "Is that why you came to me?" he asked candidly.

"Who knows?" Jaron shrugged. "I thought I was just on an adventure." He gazed off at the mountain in the afternoon sun. "I just wanted to get to the mountain." He turned back to the old man. The lines on James's face looked softer now. Jaron wasn't sure if it was early twilight or a dawning inner sensitivity, but either way, James looked younger, more vulnerable. Jaron felt different too. He'd made a friend. Experience had bonded them. "In some mysterious way we're all connected, aren't we, my friend?" he said quietly, reaching for James's shoulder. "Thanks again. I won't forget you."

"Me too you." James's voice was tender. He held Jaron's hand to steady him as he slipped over the side of the boat.

The water was waist-deep. Jaron moved toward shore. As he stepped into the foam on the shoreline, he turned and waved. James was already fumbling with the motor. As he looked up one last time, the entire scene precipitously popped and crackled. Light flashed across the sky, and Jaron dissolved in a swirl of light right before the eyes of the old man.

CHAPTER 8

Tara's Message

Jaron remolecularized in the prebirth briefing room. He was standing at the front of the class, gazing down at the arms on his body suit as his cells reconvened. In simultaneous awareness, both he and the class realized what was happening. The group burst into spontaneous clapping, but it was Élan who jumped up and moved to the front of the room.

"You're right, Élan." Jaron felt the immediate connection. "The loss of identity down there is amazing! You really do forget who you are." He was still a bit shaky from the molecular change. "My mind was hazy, and I kept getting pulled into the swirl of the old man's insecurities." He glanced over Élan's shoulder at Brooke. "I'm sure I would have missed all of you if I had remembered you, but the entire memory of all relationships was wiped from my mind. There was nothing before my immediate Earth experience. It's amazing to be so short-sighted!" he added.

"You did great," Élan countered, hugging Jaron. There was an affinity between them now.

"I thought so too," said Elder Em from the back of the room.

"I'm not so sure how well I did," answered Jaron. "I have to admit that it was far more challenging than I expected, but I did the best I could under the circumstances. I kept going in and out of the amnesia, experiencing periods of unconsciousness and then moments of unusual clarity in which I was completely aware and lucid." Jaron leaned against the elder's desk as he continued his analysis. "Now that I think about it, the inner connection almost always happened when I felt powerless and asked for help."

"But what if Jaron hadn't remembered to ask?" Brooke's dark brown eyes were pensive as she looked back at the elder from her fourth-row seat. "Would he have been on his own?"

"You're never really alone in life, Brooke, even if it feels that way sometimes." Elder Em moved toward her desk as he spoke. "As long as you're doing what's right, you'll always be supported, but a critical key to getting help along the way is remembering to ask for it. Because of the free will factor, the One waits in the wings on the stage of life until invited in."

"But I think the training really helps, Elder Em," Jaron asserted. "I could tell it was the training because of the difference between the old man's perception and mine." Jaron paused, considering the distinction. "Even though I went in and out of consciousness, my intention was stronger."

"Is that due to the training, Elder Em?" Élan cut in.

"Could be." Elder Em nodded thoughtfully. "I was monitoring both of your moments of clarity in relationship to your memory lapses during each of your simulations. You both did much better than most of the human beings we've observed."

"So you've monitored some of the other human beings?" Élan asked with sudden intense interest.

Startled by the shift in energy, Elder Em answered slowly, "Yes . . ." he answered slowly, still unsure of what Élan was alluding to. "The Welcoming Committee is monitoring many others."

"Have you monitored *the others*?"

"What others are you talking about, Élan?"

"The others, the ones who went to Earth before us." Élan's features were pained.

"Oh," he said quietly. "You mean Rhea, don't you?"

"I do so miss her," Élan blurted out unexpectedly. "I think about her a lot since we've been in training, and I can't help but wonder how she's doing."

"I understand," Elder Em answered with quiet certainty. "Love is a very special gift," he said. "And your love for Rhea will eventually bring you together again."

Zendar leaned forward in his seat, listening intently to the Elder's words. He too missed Rhea. He wished with all his heart that the three of them would be together again.

"When?" Élan pushed the elder. "When will we be together again?"

"I'm not sure. But love will always find a way." He turned to include the rest of the students in the room as he spoke. "I know that many of you have friends that have gone before."

Everyone was listening intently to the exchange between Élan and Elder Em with personal interest. "Let me settle your minds on the issue of your friends," he said. "In almost every case your love will bring you back together. The only time that loved ones don't find each other is when there's a greater lesson to be learned somewhere else on the planet." A wave of disappointment went through the room. "But even then," he encouraged, "love is like a magnet. When it's strong enough, it draws the loved ones together." The elder closed firmly. "Trust the process," he said. "There is a plan. It will all work out, I promise!"

Jaron glanced over at Brooke, silently hoping that their friendship was part of the plan. He knew better than to assume anything, but he prayed that their paths would cross on the other side some day.

Still unsettled, Élan pressed the elder. "So if you're monitoring them, how are they doing down there?"

"They're going in and out of consciousness in the same way you and Jaron did, Élan. Only they haven't had any training, so they're having a lot more difficulty." Élan's face was distressed. "It's all right, Élan. We're working with them."

"How?"

"We're reaching them through dreams." He smiled, thinking of Tara. Élan was unaware that he was leading them into the next part of the training.

"What do you mean?"

"The way you're receiving the training on this side, they're receiving their training at night during their dreams." Elder Em paused. "They're part of the plan too, you know. In fact everyone is part of the plan," he said, opening his arms as if to include the entire room. "You see the plan is bigger than all of us. It includes each and every human being, whether they know it or not. Everyone is special, and every individual has a special role to fulfill. If everyone just remembers that, and plays their part well, the plan will unfold perfectly."

"Thanks," Élan relaxed, leaning back against the elder's desk.

"These exchanges help everyone, Élan." The elder moved toward the front of the room where the two young men were standing. "Always remember to ask. It's the third mantra," he said turning to face the class. "Ask for everything, help, answers, solutions. Just ask, for asking is a creative act that generates an energy equal to your need. Answers and solutions will always follow."

"Then I have a question." Jaron looked at the elder who was standing only a few feet from him now. "It seems to me that James was hypnotized by his past.

A singular failure caused an emotional paralysis, and from that time on he created his present and future out of that solitary past incident."

"Outstanding analysis, Jaron." The elder had not expected that level of precision in his student's thinking. He was obviously pleased.

"But the question is, Elder Em, is this type of thing indicative of human behavior? Like Élan, sir, I felt as if the simulation has a much deeper significance than originally meets the eye."

The elder smiled. He couldn't have asked for a better segue into the next section. "If you'll take your seats," he said, gesturing to Élan and Jaron, "we'll gladly answer your question."

The two of them nodded and headed for their seats. As Élan slipped into his chair next to Zendar, the familiar crackle of energy flashed in the front of the room. Again a wave of warmth flooded the atmosphere as Raoul materialized beside Elder Em. The class responded to his presence as that of a long-awaited friend. A spontaneous surge of love filled the room.

"Let me pick up the thread of Jaron's question." Raoul raised his right arm as he moved into the conversation. "Jaron's intuitions regarding human behavior are accurate." Élan leaned forward in his seat, mesmerized once more by the same fathomless energy.

"There are really two climatic conditions on Earth," Raoul continued. "The first, which you experienced in Élan's simulation, is physical. The second, which we experienced in the last simulation, is mental-emotional." Shifting his weight, Raoul continued as Elder Em pulled his chair over to the wall and took a seat. "You will soon discover that preparing each of you for Earth's physical atmosphere was the easiest part of our task. As Jaron has discovered, it is Earth's mental climate that presents our greatest educational challenge."

Élan touched his arm, remembering his lacerations. His wounds had stayed with him a long time. What was Raoul alluding to? Was there a pain greater than this?

"This mental-emotional climate, known as the Human Condition, is a direct result of the human ego. Acting like a lens, the ego colors reality." Raoul's long gray robe swirled at his feet as he stepped into the area in front of Élan and Zendar. "This ego-lens, with its highly individualized viewpoint, distorts the truth, so that most people have lost sight of what it really means to be a human being. Like James, they have forgotten who they really are and why they're on the Earth." Élan felt as if Raoul was addressing him directly. "As a result, they have diminished themselves and their own capabilities and, as you will see in the next simulation, they have also diminished each other."

With a gentle flick of his wrist, Raoul gestured to the space alongside him as he spoke. Immediately the ethers began to coalesce. At first the form was subtle translucent silver shimmering on the edge of reality. Then an elegant woman materialized before them. She was tall and refined, her thick dark brown hair curled slightly at the ends resting on her shoulders.

"Please welcome Tara." Raoul reached for Tara's hand and raised it in a ceremonial presentation to the group. She was wearing an ivory-colored floor-length robe of a satiny silk that glistened slightly as Raoul moved her arm in the light. Her dark eyes were filled with empathy. "Tara is also a member of the Committee," Raoul continued. "She is responsible for the destiny of children, and she guides and counsels those who work with them. Elder Em and I have asked her to join us today because of our increasing concern regarding the children of Earth."

None of the group had expected this. A gentle, settling effect filled the room with Tara's presence. An aura of peace surrounded her. Élan relaxed back in his seat, touched by her gentleness and warmth. For a long moment no one moved in the room. Mesmerized by Tara's serenity, they sat as if enchanted, absorbing this new vibration.

"My friends," Tara said, stepping forward to speak to the group, "I come before you as a member of the Committee that has been working to assist the children of Earth." Her voice was clear with a round melodic tone. The students were completely spellbound. "This Human Condition that Raoul has spoken of has been handed down from one generation to the next through a process called 'imprinting.' Thus it has affected every child born on the planet.

"Today more souls are being born on Earth than ever before." As she moved into the middle aisle, Élan could see that her beauty and gentility were tempered by a subtle command. "Beautiful beings, like yourselves, are entering the planet seeking the learning and growth available in Earth's curriculum," she said. "However, before these beings have an opportunity to remember who they are, they are becoming caught in the web of unconscious conditioning. Imprinted by those in the environment around them, they are finding themselves powerless to fight the amnesia."

Tara's eyes were soft as she continued. "When some of these young beings do sense that something is wrong and try to rebel, the adults in their environment react to the rebellion. Instead of reading the message between the lines, the adults are reacting to the symptoms, ignoring the cause. These young ones are calling out for help, but few are listening." Tara's voice carried an authority now, and her presence filled the room. "Instead, people are closing their eyes to the issues, educational budgets are being cut and funds diverted to other programs. Governments have turned a deaf ear to the needs of children, and by so doing they have forsaken the well-being of the nations."

Raoul, who was standing behind Tara watching the faces of the students, suddenly spoke up. "The adults are too entangled in the web of unconsciousness to help their own children. They are mesmerized by the same spell that was passed onto them."

"Like James." Jaron was clear, his tone was conclusive. "I'm sure that his mother had no intention of hurting him. She loved him, but she unconsciously acted out her insecurities and fears. She did it so well that James ended up living them out."

"Exactly," Tara said.

"So you've been watching our simulations?" Jaron asked.

"The entire Welcoming Committee has been with you from the start."

"And your intention," Élan interjected, "is to break the cycle of imprinting?"

"Actually," Tara turned to address Élan directly, "the cycle on Earth is starting to break now, Élan, but the birth of a new consciousness takes time. Our intention is to flood the Earth with souls like you, souls who have gone through the training and can maintain a steady, and hopefully unbroken, awareness of who they are." Tara surveyed the group as she reiterated Elder Em's teaching. "You must each train yourselves well, for your effectiveness on the other side will depend on the amount of practice you put in here. Then, just as Jaron helped James, you will be able to help others by the power of your awareness. This will accelerate the process of awakening and move the planet ever more rapidly toward critical mass."

Élan's imagination was captivated. "So there's a destiny to be fulfilled."

"That there is." Tara smiled and glanced over at Elder Em who was watching the exchange from the sidelines silently pleased. They both knew that these qualities of enthusiasm and personal insight would someday be Élan's greatest gifts.

"Soon," Élan added quietly.

"Soon, Élan," Tara confirmed, "when you're born, actually. That's what all of this preparation is leading to, you know."

"It's time for us to say good-bye." Raoul's voice gently intruded on the conversation.

"When will we see you again?" Ashley looked up at Tara standing just a few feet from her desk.

"Later," she answered elusively.

"When?" Ashley insisted.

Tara smiled at Ashley's tenacity. "I'll be working with all of you during your formative years on Earth." She deliberated a moment and then added, "For others among you, I will also be there later, for I guide those who work with children."

Élan was silent, his hazel green eyes riveted on Tara. Was there a subliminal message in her words? His future flashed momentarily across the horizon of his awareness, but it was just beyond reach. What would it hold? Where would he be? Glancing over at Zendar, he hoped the two of them would be together. Zendar caught his eye. He too was feeling the import of the moment.

"Remember that you are loved," Tara said, walking to the front of the room to stand beside Raoul as she spoke.

"And study well," Raoul added, "for as our friend Élan said in his own way, soon each of you will be stepping into the pages of destiny." With that Raoul gestured in Tara's direction and the two turned, simultaneously bowing slightly in an acknowledgment of completion. The ethers began to flicker as Raoul and Tara began a stunning slow dissolve. Silver violet shimmered through their cells as their solid forms turned to translucent rose and disappeared into the ethers.

Staring at the space where Tara and Raoul had been standing, Élan was reflective. He wondered if the others felt the same way he did in their presence. Silently observing the room, he noticed Brooke glancing over at Ashley. It was obvious that they were both moved.

Ashley looked up briefly in response. The force of Tara's message had touched her, for it came not through her words but through her being. She prayed to be like her someday.

"It is time for a break." The elder's voice broke through their reverie. "We'll meet back here after you complete your next three mantras."

CHAPTER 9

The Human Condition

"What do you think, Zen?" Élan had suggested they invite Jaron to join them. His insights had been decisive, and three heads might be better than two. "Besides, Jaron might be experiencing a dose of the human condition and maybe we could help him."

"Great idea!"

"Detour then?" Élan grabbed his friend's arm and the two spun around headed in the opposite direction, intent on finding Jaron's cubicle.

The door swung wide on the first knock and Jaron's perceptive dark eyes greeted them. "What are you two doing here?" he asked in shocked surprise.

"How come you answered the door so quickly?" Élan countered.

"I was on my way out." Jaron was holding his manual in his left hand. "I had just reached for the door handle when your knock came." His right hand was still on the doorknob. "You caught me off guard. What can I do for you?"

"Élan suggested that you might want to join us," Zendar offered.

"To study?" Jaron asked. Zendar nodded. "Love to, but I was on my way to Brooke's. We agreed to study together again."

"She's welcome too," said Élan. "I thought we might cover more ground if there were two of us with some Earth experience."

"Sounds good!" Jaron shook his head. Suddenly pensive he added, "I have to admit that I was really shaken down there. The fact that I made it was either luck or the grace of God."

"I felt the same way," Élan confirmed. "Any signs of withdrawal?"

"Not yet. In fact I'm feeling more committed than ever. But after my trial run, I'm not sure any of us could ever study enough." Jaron thought for a moment. "Tell you what, I'll see if Brooke wants to come. If she does, we'll be there shortly. If not, I'll stop by and let you know."

"Good," Élan nodded. He and Zendar disappeared down the corridor in the direction of his sleep chamber. Jaron rounded the bend at the other end of the hall, bound for Brooke's room.

Jaron rejoined the two a few minutes later with Brooke at his side. Deciding not to waste any time, they each found a comfortable place in the room. Jaron offered to read out loud and they settled down to their studies together.

• • •

THE MATOS MANTRAS

Be Still
(4)

Be still, breathe, and go within. Turn not your attention outward to the world. For on Earth, the world goes on world-ing and life goes on life-ing, as the ego continues its play.

Dive deep, down beneath the ripples of the mind, and enter the secret chamber of the heart. Withdraw your attention, and dwell in the solitude and silence for a short period daily.

Be still, and out of the silence will come your knowing. Be still, and out of the stillness will come the direction for your journey. Be still, and the One will guide you. Be still, and you will remember who you are and who all others are around you.

See
(5)

See all life through the eyes of the heart. The eye that sees from the heart has both the keen perception of discernment as well as the soft sight of compassion. This combination of hard and soft, strong yet ever yielding, firm but ever gentle gives perfect sight to the seer.

Develop the sacred gift of inner sight, for herein lies both the ability to recognize truth as well as the capacity to see the One that lives in the heart of every being.

Sweet is the vision seen with the eye of the heart for it is lit by the light of the soul.

Act
(6)

Act in a way that honors all, for what you do comes back to you. The law of cause and effect is the check and balance system for the entire universe.

Ask yourself, would I want to be treated the way I am treating? Would I want to be dealt with the way I am dealing? Would I want to be loved the way I am expressing love at this moment?

If the answer to all of these questions is yes, than act! Act in a way that furthers all, raises all, and honors all, for what we do to others we are really doing to ourselves.

Élan's voice trailed off as he completed the sixth mantra. Closing his book, he jumped down from his window seat to take the lead. "Who's going to be tested, my friends?" He said looking around at each of them.

"I'll pass for now," Brooke said. She was still thinking of Tara. Something about her presence had moved her deeply.

"I'll go first!" Zendar volunteered, unaware of her reaction.

"BE STILL, SEE, ACT . . . Where do you want to begin?" Élan paced, manual in hand.

"I think the three are connected." Zendar sat forward and closed his manual. "But I'll take the first one."

"OK." Élan leaned against the ledge and crossed his arms. "Be still, my friend, what does that mantra mean to you?"

Jaron smiled to himself. Their friendship was indeed special. He looked over at Brooke who was observing their interaction closely.

Zendar crossed his legs and turned to face his friend who was looking down at him from an angle at the end of the bed. "That's a deep one Élan." He paused and stared at the floor as if to catch the thread of his thinking. "On this side of the window all things are known," he began slowly. "There are no hidden meanings. Everything is clearly visible, because everything is light."

Zendar stood and began to pace. "On Earth, however, not all things are visible. It seems to me that there are two worlds within the world of one down there."

Élan looked puzzled. "I'm not sure I understand what you're saying. Explain!"

Zendar continued pacing. "First, there is the outer world, a world that is noisy and loud, metaphorically speaking. I mean, there is a lot going on in Earth's outer world: color, sound, physical 'reality,' as it were. This outer world vies for our attention, yet it is not the place that peace comes from." He stopped when he reached the wall and turned. "Peace comes from within: the world within the heart and mind of a human being. This is the important world, for it is the place where answers can be heard, and insights seen."

"What does that have to do with being still?" Élan asked.

"In order to contact this inner world, two skills are necessary: concentration and focus. Both of these are aspects of the fourth mantra, 'Be Still.' We have to concentrate and stop the chatter in our minds. Then we have to focus our attention within. All knowledge and wisdom comes from our ability to do this. Yet this is probably one of the much-forgotten secrets on Earth."

"How do you know that it's a much-forgotten secret when you haven't even been there?" Élan was curious.

"Well I was with you on your venture." Zendar looked at Élan as he spoke. "And I also watched James's reactions closely during your venture, Jaron." "One particular thing became very evident as I observed him."

"What was that?" Jaron asked.

"That he'd lost contact with his inner world. He had been infused with a dream as a young person, but when the outer world rebuffed him and a storm challenged his intention, he lost sight of his vision. Forgetting to renew himself within, he lost his hope. His face was etched in sadness because he no longer heard his inner song, the song of his own soul."

"You're right." Jaron saw the old man's face as Zendar spoke.

"So," Zendar said, "if James would be still and focus his attention within for a few moments each day, he'd soon get in touch with himself again."

"How do you mean?" Still buoyant from Tara's visit, Brooke was back in the conversation again.

Zendar was thoughtful. He hadn't expected to be pushed on this point. "Meditation and prayer," he answered finally. "These are two methods of stilling the mind so that we can experience the silent song of the soul, spirit whispering within." He leaned forward looking at Brooke as he continued. "I think we'd see a different man if he did a little bit of that daily, ten minutes a day even."

"In what way?" Brooke asked, fascinated now by the depth of Zendar's perception.

"I think he'd have a new zest for life," Zendar answered.

"Even at his age?"

"Hope is ageless, Brooke, and hope would be rekindled in his heart."

Jaron was impressed. "That was good, Zen." He too was fascinated with Zendar's approach.

"Furthermore," Zendar continued, "this daily practice would have strengthened James's ability to be still in the middle of a crisis, represented by the storm. That's what happened to you, Jaron. For a moment you were able to concentrate and stop your mind." Zendar turned and sat on the edge of the bed facing Jaron. "As a result, in the middle of chaos, you were able to disconnect. You entered the place of your own stillness and stopped the world."

"How did you know?" Jaron was taken aback.

"I watched you. It was written all over your face. The moment you shifted your attention away from the storm and focused on asking within, you severed your attachment to the world. It no longer had any power over you and the fear disappeared from your face."

Although not amazed at his friend's astute dissertation, Élan lowered his eyes so that Jaron wouldn't see the depth of his pride. Zendar was his dearest friend, ever insightful, deep and even penetrating in the precision of his understanding of the human heart and mind. Élan often wondered where Zendar got his power of observation. Maybe he would never know. Élan silently pulled himself back up onto the ledge and glanced out of the window, momentarily wishing Rhea was with them. The three of them had always been so good together. They continually challenged each other's thinking, and it seemed to bring the best out in all of them.

Encouraged by Zendar's clarity, Brooke volunteered to take the fifth mantra. She described the "eye of the heart" as a kind of metaphorical riddle that alluded to deeper meanings. Using Jaron's encounter with James as an example, she related Jaron's insight in the boat to the feelings and intuition of the heart.

"It's like what Tara and Raoul shared," she concluded. "When we use the gift of inner sight, we are able to cut through the facade of the Human Condition. That's exactly what you did with James. You saw behind the social conditioning to the light within.

"One more thing," Brooke added. "I noticed myself hedging during your simulation. I felt uncomfortable when you pushed James a couple of times. You were courageous in your approach."

"On the outside," Jaron laughed. "But inside I came close to giving it up more than once." Jaron looked right through Brooke as he spoke. "I went through moments of apathy myself." He felt as if he was in the boat again, fighting the storm and trying to deal with James's reactions at the same time. "I got impatient with James and even wanted to quit at one point." He laughed. "Good thing I had amnesia. If I'd been aware that I was in a simulation, I would have asked to be beamed back up!"

"A simulation isn't over until it's over, is it?" Élan laughed.

"Guess not," Jaron reflected.

"Mine wasn't," Élan added.

Jaron saw Élan's face as he was swept under a second time during the height of the storm. "Got the point," he said, remembering how he had wished that Elder Em would save him.

"No way out but through." Jaron was staring at the floor. "I think that's the secret to the sixth mantra, Act," he said. "You might as well act in alignment with the highest purpose because there's no way out of an experience until you go all the way through it."

"That's what the elder was trying to say to Ashley." Brooke's eyes flashed with insight. "He said that an experience repeats itself until we get the lesson." She paused. "Trial and error method, he called it."

"I guess mastery of anything comes in stages." Jaron paused. "It's a process, isn't it?" He looked at Zendar thoughtfully and added, "Maybe that's why your suggestion of daily prayer and meditation would be so powerful. It would allow our learning and growth to occur in stages."

"It seems that process is what the Earth is all about," Zendar said softly. He was touched.

Brooke was quiet. Élan stared out the window. He felt the insight in his stomach. Jaron gazed at the wall. The room was completely silent. Nobody spoke for a long time.

When they did it was only to say good-bye. They hugged and agreed that they would see each other back in class. Each felt the affinity between them.

Élan closed the door behind Jaron and Brooke. "Special souls," he reflected. "That was a great exchange."

"Far better than I could have imagined," Zendar agreed. "Glad you suggested it." He walked over to the window and stared out in rapt thought.

"Try it."

"What?"

"The window ledge." Élan said. Zendar looked at him quizzically. "Go on," he said sitting on the bed.

Zendar pulled himself up into Élan's seat and turned to place his feet against the window frame so that he was facing the bed.

"No wonder you like this spot," he said, gazing out of the window. "It's so safe here."

"It *is* special," Élan nodded in agreement.

For a few moments they were both lost in thought. Suddenly Élan felt Zendar's distance and looked up. His eyes were glazed and he had a faraway look on his face. Élan couldn't help but stare at him. Zendar's profile was stunning, a perfectly straight nose above a strong jaw. Even from the side, Zendar's eyes were electric.

Élan wondered where his friend had mentally gone. Sensing Élan's look, Zendar sighed and turned toward him. "I was visualizing a perfect life," he said. "I'd like it to be one of service."

Élan felt it too. "That would be nice," he said. To be able to express the love that he felt, that would be sheer joy. His heart was full and he wanted to share that fullness with others. "I wonder what a life of service looks like."

"I'm not sure what it looks like yet, but I can feel it."

"Maybe if we review the text one more time, we'll get a stronger sense of it."

"I'm with you."

The two of them stood to stretch and then returned to their normal positions. Élan went back to his window and Zendar lay on the bed. They both began to read.

Chapter 10

Streetwise

Élan looked up as Elder Em entered the room a few minutes later. The Elder now wore a full-length gray robe identical to the one that Raoul had worn earlier. Élan couldn't take his eyes off him; what a distinct difference in demeanor. His silver hair flowed gracefully around his face, resting on the rim of the hood. The entire effect was to accent the elder's stunning soft green eyes. They looked iridescent as he turned his head in the light. Élan was in awe, seeing for the first time what he had not seen before.

Elder Em was not the usual teacher. This extraordinary being had worn the violet outfit earlier to make his students feel comfortable in their first stages of training. He was willing to be one with them during the initial awkward phase of receiving a body suit.

All eyes followed the elder's movements. Except for the gentle swish of the elder's robe as it brushed against his legs, a profound hush filled the room. Élan leaned forward to catch Jaron's face. He too was captivated, staring in rapt attention at the elder as he moved through the room.

Fully aware of the impact his change in dress had made, Elder Em paced his movements. Allowing the lesson to linger in the atmosphere, he stopped momentarily to chat quietly with different students as he passed their desks. Finally he approached the front of the room and turned to face the students from a spot beside his desk.

"Are there any questions on the new mantras before we begin with the next section of training?" His eyes fell on Ashley who was staring at the floor. "How about you, Ashley?" He moved toward her as he spoke.

Ashley looked up in wide-eyed disbelief as he stepped beside her desk. Was he reading her thoughts? She had wanted to volunteer for a simulation ever since Tara's visit.

"I don't have any questions, Elder Em."

"But you do want to go?" he encouraged, reaching his hand out in her direction.

"Yes." Ashley said quietly accepting his hand. After all she had reviewed each lesson thoroughly, committing all of them to heart. She even secretly wished that she might be able to maintain the unbroken awareness that Tara had spoken of earlier.

"Come on, then." Elder Em gently squeezed her hand as she stood and they walked together to the front of the room.

Justin was watching the exchange with keen interest. His mind reeled as he watched the two walking to the front of the class.

"Elder Em," he burst out impulsively.

"Yes, Justin?"

"Are you sending Ashley down there alone?"

"Well, that was the idea."

"How come?"

Ashley looked on in surprise. She'd never really noticed Justin before.

"What do you mean, 'how come?' " Elder Em asked in surprise. "Do you have another suggestion?"

"Well, you never gave the rest of us a chance to volunteer." Justin appeared spurned.

"Did you want to go?" He looked over at Ashley, who gave a barely perceptible nod of acquiescence.

"Well I'd thought about it." Justin still feigned nonchalance.

"And what had you come up with?"

"Well . . ." Justin stammered. "Well, maybe Ashley should have a partner," he blurted out. "After all, the Committee never sent two representatives down there together! It might be a good opportunity to test a new approach!"

Elder Em's eyes twinkled as he watched Justin's mental gymnastics. "A new kind of test . . . I never thought of it, Justin!"

Justin nodded confidently. "So I thought I might go along with Ashley. Maybe we could support each other."

"How do you feel about it?" Elder Em looked down at Ashley standing beside him.

"I can handle that," Ashley answered, silently curious about the turn of events.

"Decided then." Elder Em nodded. "Come on up here, Justin."

Justin nearly fell out of his seat in anticipation. Quickly regaining his composure, he stood, stretched his shoulders, and walked to the front of the room poised. Ashley blinked as a flicker of surprise shot through her. She felt immediately drawn to him.

Standing with Ashley on one arm and Justin on the other, the elder addressed the group. "In this simulation you will discover what happens when a society has lost its soul. Justin and Ashley will be facing one of the greatest challenges on Earth at this time. Their adventure centers around the anger and rage that ensues when love, values, and purpose have been undermined and the family unit impaired."

Justin glanced over at Ashley. Although he wasn't sure that he understood all of the elder's words, he was glad to be going with her. There was something special about her.

"Ashley and Justin will begin where Élan and Jaron left off." The elder nodded to the two of them as he spoke. "Naturally your goal is the same. You'll approach the mountain from a slightly different angle than the two of them, but you will still be on a journey in search of the cave."

He paused for a moment. "Because learning is cumulative you'll both maintain an unbroken continuity of consciousness with both Élan's and Jaron's learning.

"Now for a clothing change," he said, moving away from the two of them as he spoke. "Earth clothes," he said, snapping his fingers in their direction.

Élan and Jaron eyed each other as the two were transformed. Their own experiences were still vivid as they viewed Justin's light green shirt and black pants. Ashley was dressed in a soft turquoise blouse and blue jeans.

Both looked down at their arms in surprise. It was the watch on their wrists. Élan smiled remembering the first sensations of constriction again.

Reaching into his drawer, Elder Em pulled out a blue wallet and handed it to Ashley. "You'll find your identification inside," he said in answer to her puzzled look. "It's one of Earth's requirements," he added, reaching into his drawer again. "This one is for you," he said handing a black wallet to Justin. As Justin took it he continued, "You'll find money for your journey in there, as well as your identification and several credit cards that will make your Earth visit easier."

Justin opened the wallet to find his picture on the ID card. He was suddenly shaken, "How did you know it was going to be me?"

"We just knew," the elder answered quietly, his eyes gazing steadily into the young man's eyes. Justin blinked, trying to recapture his poise. He should have known.

Next Elder Em reached alongside the desk and picked up two small backpacks. "Inside you'll find traveling clothes and others items to make your stay there comfortable." Handing one to each of them, he added, "Are you ready?"

Placing his wallet in the zippered compartment on the outside of his pack, Justin took a deep breath. "I'm ready," he said looking over at Ashley. "How about you?"

She dropped her wallet into the main compartment of her backpack and nodded. "Ready," she said confidently.

Elder Em moved to the panel on the front board.

"So now," he continued, "imagine that we have arrived at Brenton, a small city approximately two hundred miles from the base of Mount Akros."

"Is that where we begin?" Justin felt an unexpected hesitancy at the reality of what was occurring. Everything had moved so quickly since he'd stood up. He hoped he'd made the right decision. If it weren't for Ashley he wouldn't be going at all. "But she is going," he thought decisively. The choice had been made.

"That's where you'll begin," answered the Elder. "Brenton, a small metropolis of approximately a million people." Ashley's legs were suddenly weak. She reached for the elder's arm.

"It's all right," he said reassuringly. "Use the

mantra of stillness and the gift of inner sight. Consider before you act, and everything will work out for the two of you." Ashley nodded.

Justin straightened his shoulders. "I'm ready, sir," he said, looking into Elder Em's eyes, his voice now firm with conviction.

With that, the Elder made the familiar move of his hand to the button on the panel, and the well-known hiss and crackle split the air. Justin and Ashley dissolved in a vortex of light that swirled and spun upwards like a funnel, bursting in the air.

The scene exploded on a suburban street as a city bus swung around the corner and headed down the road out of sight. There was still a black trail of exhaust fumes in the air as Justin and Ashley molecularized.

Ashley had landed with one foot on the sidewalk and one on the dark black asphalt. She almost fell over as she tried to rebalance with the weight of her backpack.

Justin was standing staring down at himself as his cells reconvened in the middle of the road. Just then a car raced around the corner. He jumped back and tripped, falling in Ashley's direction as the car swerved to avoid him. The driver screamed and raised his fist as he sped by. Justin stared in shocked disbelief at the intensity of the anger. He'd never experienced anything like it before.

"Are you all right?" Ashley asked, rushing to his side.

"I sure feel clumsy," he said, reaching to recover his pack from the side of the road. Dusting the dirt from his pants, he examined his left hand. It was scraped and bleeding slightly.

"It wasn't your fault. He was going too fast."

Justin walked over to the sidewalk with Ashley. He was trying to recover his composure as he rubbed his hand to remove the particles of gravel that had imbedded in the skin on his palm.

His legs felt wobbly as the two of them stood on the side of the road. "What a welcome."

Gazing down the street, he noticed the symmetry of the area for the first time. Rows of small shade trees lined the grass at the edge of the sidewalk as far as he could see in both directions. Purple and pink flowers were planted at the base of every tree lining the road, lending a refreshing, clean look to the neighborhood.

Following an intuitive urge, Justin nodded in the direction of the setting sun, and they began walking.

Shades of sunset soon dappled the neighborhood, turning the rooftops into amber. Subtle shadows slipped across a mackerel sky as night entered and daylight surrendered to shades of evening purple. The air was becoming cooler. For a long time they walked silently side by side, lost in their own personal observations of Earth.

"We need to find a place to eat," Ashley said, finally breaking the silence. She was beginning to feel hungry and nervous about where they were. They were strangers in a place they'd never been and night was falling.

He nodded as they arrived at a corner and stopped to consider their direction. It was nearly dark now. The streetlights flickered and then lit up in a twinkling line that seemed to extend infinitely to their left and right. Down the lane to their left they spotted a series of differently designed buildings, most were two-stories high and tightly bunched together. "What do you think?" Justin signaled to the left as he spoke. His stomach was growling. Ashley nodded in agreement, and they rounded the corner headed in the direction of the two-story structures a few blocks away.

A few minutes later a middle-aged woman appeared dragging a large plastic trash container out of a darkened garage directly in front of him. Justin moved quickly to help her. Lifting the trash can, he placed it on the sidewalk. She thanked him and confirmed their direction. The center of town was about half a mile from them. There they would find restaurants and inns. "Look for a two-story red brick building nestled at the end of a circular driveway on the left about half a mile from here," the woman said, pointing straight ahead in the direction they were heading.

"She was right," Justin said about ten minutes

later. He was pointing to an old brick building set in a circular drive to their left. "We couldn't have missed it if we had tried."

They registered at the inn, and after a meal in the café next door both retired to their rooms. They agreed to meet in the lobby at eight the next morning for coffee. Each slipped into their own private dream time where the fresh sights and sounds of their Earth experience could be refined into a new reality.

The next morning, Justin held a cup of coffee out to Ashley as she entered the lobby. "Hi."

"Morning," she replied taking the cup from his outstretched hand. "Thanks," she said walking over to the couch. She seemed distant.

"How are you doing?"

"OK."

"Well how come it doesn't feel that way?"

"I had a dream," she said seating herself.

"Tell me about it." He walked over and handed her a cranberry muffin on a napkin.

"Thanks." She placed her coffee on the table in front of her and took the muffin from him. "We were in a city looking for a way out," she continued.

"That wasn't a dream," he said, sitting in a matching love seat facing the window. "That was reality."

"Don't tease. It could be important," she said, nibbling on the edge of the muffin. "You and I were walking down a street looking for a landmark, something with a clue. We came to a corner crossing and suddenly everything felt ominous, strange. There were faces, taunting us." Ashley shuddered at the memory.

"Then what?"

"I remember feeling trapped, like there was no way out." She gazed off at the floor in front of her.

"Go on."

"Then my morning wake-up call came." She shrugged slightly. "I lost the rest of it."

"Hmm. What do you think it means?"

"I'm not sure. But it didn't feel good," she said, looking at him directly. "The wake-up call was a relief. I wanted out of that dream."

"Maybe it was just one of those mixed-up nightmares." He wanted to take away her anguish. "Maybe it's just that we're in a strange town with new sights and all."

"Maybe." Ashley was reflective. She wasn't so sure. "It left me feeling very strange."

"How are you feeling now?"

"A little better, thanks." She smiled and reached for her coffee. "It always feels better to talk about it." The two of them slipped into silence, finishing their coffee and muffins, and gazing out of the panoramic front window. The morning sun was still hidden, but its signature was visible in golden shafts that splintered the eastern sky. Across the street and behind the inn, billowy white clouds were etched in silver.

"That's quite a sight isn't it?" Justin, who rarely showed his inner feelings, pointed at the morning sky, obviously touched.

"It sure is." Ashley nodded. She was sitting to Justin's right so that he could see her as well as the window beyond. He had never had a chance to observe her before. This was a welcome opportunity. She was sitting directly in his line of vision, and he couldn't help but look at her.

Her movements were smooth and graceful. There was a certain serenity about her as she sipped her coffee and gazed at the changing sky. As he watched her closely, he realized that she wasn't the delicate lady that she first appeared to be. He sensed an inner resilience about her, an illusive quality, refined and graceful on the outside yet a kind of steely stamina within. There was a stillness in the aura around her. He felt peaceful in her presence. It stabilized him somehow.

"Unusual combination," he thought.

"Do you think we should get a map of the area?" she asked and turned to look at him. Her hazel brown eyes smiled from within.

"Probably. Let me ask at the desk." Justin walked to the registration counter in the lobby and rang the bell. A young man appeared in the doorway.

"Yes sir," he said walking up to the counter. He was a bit shorter than Justin with ash blond hair. He had a clean look about him. Justin liked him immediately.

"What can I do for you?" he asked.

"Do you have a map of the area?"

"Sure," he said, bending to open the cabinet behind the counter.

"I thought we had some maps," he said, shuffling through the printed material on the shelves. "But I think we're out of them." He stood and dusted his hand on his pant leg. "I'm sorry, we seem to have everything except a map. There's a Gas-o-Mat three blocks down the street to your right. Why don't you try there."

Finishing their light breakfast they retrieved their backpacks from their rooms and checked out of the inn. Sounds of morning traffic exploded around them as they entered the street and headed in the direction the clerk had suggested. It was a four-lane boulevard lined with motels and small shops. The aroma of pastry and coffee drifted out of the restaurant they had eaten in the night before. Here and there along the street people were in various stages of preparation for a new day.

Three blocks passed quickly and they arrived at the convenience market.

"Why don't you go get the map," Ashley said as she took the packs and walked over to the bus bench in front of the gas station. "I'll wait for you here."

Justin returned a few minutes later with a couple of maps. "Nothing is free around here," he commented as he sat down beside her.

"Did we need two of them?"

"Just a hunch, I guess. One is a street map. The other is a map of the surrounding vicinity. That's the one I'm interested in."

"Why?"

"I'm not sure." He began unfolding the panels on his knees. "We had to have a street map, but I had an instinctive feeling about this area map." He shrugged. "Don't know what it is, but I trust it."

Ashley was comfortable with him. She always trusted her intuition too. As she began silently studying the map over Justin's shoulder, a tingling sensation began in her stomach. "You're right," she said. "There's something here."

With that Justin started slowly and methodically moving his right hand up the far right side of the map. His eyes skimmed the words as he touched them. Suddenly he stopped.

"Mount Akros," he said, reading the words beneath his hand. The words sounded so familiar, but where had he heard them before? "Mount Akros," he whispered again.

Ashley blinked and gazed off into space. "What is it?" she said, turning quietly to face Justin.

Their eyes locked. Something powerful was there, right on the edge of consciousness. What was it?

Back in the course room Élan flew out of his seat. "That's the mountain," he said out loud.

"That's the mountain," Justin said quietly.

"What mountain?" Ashley was puzzled.

"The one in our quest," Élan cried.

"The one in our quest," Justin repeated hypnotically in response to Ashley's question.

"Our quest?" Ashley echoed entranced. She still felt the twinge in her stomach. "You're right though, there is something about that mountain."

Justin shook himself trying to throw off the feelings, but they persisted. "I'm not sure why, Ashley, but we have to go there. We must get to the mountain." He stood and started back to the service station office. "Be right back."

Justin returned a few minutes later waving a slip of paper in his hand. "I got directions," he said. "We're off to the mountain, Ashley! The man in there said it's easy. Only two transfers on the city bus and we'll be at the main bus depot." He sat down on the bench beside her. "From there it's a five-hour ride into the country."

Ashley took the slip of paper from him. "How long before the first bus?"

Justin looked at his watch. "Twenty minutes or so. It'll be here at nine-fifteen."

Following the directions on the paper, the two boarded bus #9. Sixteen city blocks later they exited. About fifteen minutes later bus #7 turned the corner and headed toward them.

Bus #7 was older. It lurched and rocked to a stop, brakes screeching and exhaust fumes pouring from the rear. As the driver took their transfers, Justin informed him of their stop. He nodded gruffly in reply and stepped on the gas. The bus pitched forward, throwing the two of them a few steps toward the rear. Justin grabbed the bus pole with one hand and Ashley with the other. He helped her into a seat and then swung in beside her, dropping the packs into the empty seat in front of them.

The bus was half-full with people scattered throughout the seats. The friendly feeling of bus #9 had been replaced with an edginess, a dissonant energy in the air. Justin fidgeted unconsciously, his left knee jerking nervously up and down with tension. Ashley turned to look at the inside of the bus. It was old and dirty from years of abuse. Candy wrappers were scattered on the floor, and dried soda spills dripped like long dark tears frozen in time on the backs of two of the seats ahead of them. She sensed the aggression. It was written in the graffiti of misuse splattered on the walls and seats of the bus over the years. She could feel the strain reflected in Justin's body next to her, his leg hammering the floor of the bus.

She inhaled deeply and consciously relaxed her shoulders. Withdrawing her attention, she stilled her mind in a seek and search for a landscape of like nature. Only the shadowy dream of the night before drifted across her mind. The images weren't the same, but the feelings were. Something ominous was approaching. Its foreboding hung like a huge invisible gray cloud in the atmosphere of the bus. Ashley reached over and slid her hand into Justin's. She needed his strength, and she knew he needed her stillness. Feeling her hand on his leg beneath his hand, he was suddenly aware again of his surroundings. His knee came to an immediate halt in midair. He breathed deeply, slowly lowering his leg and intentionally released his shoulders. He hadn't realized how tense he was. He looked down at Ashley, whose hazel eyes were turned nervously in his direction.

One more breath in unison and he squeezed her hand, noticing how small it was in comparison to his. Feeling immediately protective, he tried to reassure her. "We'll be all right," he said, inwardly praying it to be true.

Together they turned and looked at the seats behind them. The rear of the bus was filled with a smattering of shadowy figures murmuring quietly, punctuating their speech with sordid pronouncements. Ashley's stomach tightened. Justin increased his grip, his thigh muscle taut with apprehension.

At that moment the bus driver announced their stop. Eyeing them in the mirror, he nodded and signaled their exit with his eyes. The front doors made a rusty sound as the hinges creaked and the black rubber scraped against the bottom step as it opened. Justin grabbed their packs, and Ashley clung tightly to his arm as the two disembarked from the bus. The bus doors slammed closed behind them and the bus roared abruptly away from the curb in a dark cloud of gaseous fumes.

Justin stood watching as the bus rounded a corner

and pulled out of sight. Then he turned and looked down at Ashley who was glancing around nervously. Resigned to the situation, the two approached the bench. The area was as forbidding as the bus that had brought them there. An ominous feeling hung in the woodwork of the covering that surrounded the bench on three sides. Why hadn't the service station attendant mentioned this? Justin wondered.

Justin sat down next to Ashley and reached her hand, his mind racing. Surely the guy would have told him! Something must be wrong. Intending to check the time of the next bus, he reached into his right pocket and pulled out the slip of paper with the information on it. An icy chill ran down the back of his neck as he reread the instructions. They had just debarked from bus #7, and the paper said they should have been disembarking from bus #1. In his excitement he'd mistaken the two numbers. The street name was the same, but they probably would have exited miles away from this area.

Ashley was too engrossed in her surroundings to notice the sudden tension in his arms. She was studying the panorama in front of her. It wasn't a pretty sight. Shanty-style old brick houses lined the cross street to the left. About half a block down and across the street to the right was a Quick Stop store. It appeared to be fairly quiet at the moment. The ground around the entrance was covered with newspaper and wrappers that had been pressed against the wall by the last big gust of wind. "It looks like the inside of the bus," she thought to herself as her eyes scanned the street beyond.

Her eyes stopped suddenly on a gang of five boys at the end of the block. They talked boisterously and headed toward the bus stop. They grew louder as they approached, haranguing and mouthing off at one another. Justin turned to see what the clamor was all about just as Ashley nudged him. "My dream is coming true," she said, her throat dry and parched.

"Well it doesn't feel good."

"Neither did my dream," she replied.

And to think that they'd gotten on the wrong bus to meet it. Justin was boggled. The hand of destiny was approaching, and they'd walked into it through a blind spot! This wasn't the time to try to figure out what it all meant!

At that moment one of the boys spotted the couple. He was the shortest of the group, solid and stocky, in a tight-fitting dark blue T-shirt and a raggedy pair of jeans with a hole above the left knee. Whispering something to the others, he pointed in their direction and they turned to stare. Justin cringed, tightening the hold on Ashley's hand.

"This is it. Stay calm, Justin," she whispered. She felt sick to her stomach. It was the same feeling she had in the dream.

Darting in front of a fast-moving van, the stocky boy jumped to the sidewalk and strutted up to Justin, stopping about six feet in front of him. The others followed behind him, crossing between passing cars.

"What are you doing in our area, pretty boy?" He crossed his arms over his chest, spread his legs, and stared belligerently into Justin's eyes.

Justin, who was still seated on the bench, struggled with an appropriate response. His immediate impulse was to laugh. The little tough guy looked so funny standing there staring him in the eye. He looked small in comparison to Justin's strapping body. Then the other four swaggered up, flanking him from behind, and Justin decided that this was not a laughing matter. His size wasn't important now, he was outnumbered. These guys were serious about something, even though he couldn't figure out quite what it was.

"What do you think, guys?" the short one said, gesturing in Justin's direction.

"Give him a chance, Gino." The tallest one with "Leon" tattooed on his left arm, stepped forward. "Maybe he doesn't know the rules on our turf."

"Well then, we'll have to educate him, won't we?" Gino snickered. "Tell him the rules, Leon." His eyes were cold slate, glaring icily at the two of them.

"The rules are real simple. There's only two of them." Leon crossed his arms proudly showing his well-muscled chest and shoulders beneath a tight tank top. "Rule number one: This is our turf," he said smugly. Just then he caught a peripheral glimpse of Ashley and momentarily recoiled at her familiarity. What was it?

"You're right," Justin was apologetic. "We'll be out of here as soon as we can!"

"You don't understand, pretty boy." Another gang member with dark glowering eyes stepped forward. "This is our territory and you can't leave without hearing the rest of the rules." His voice was taunting. "Go on, Leon, finish the rules."

"Rule number two:" Leon sneered, self-contained again. "Our turf is taxed." The others laughed contemptuously, eyeing Justin's pack on the bench beside him.

The youth with the dark menacing eyes stepped to Justin's left. Snatching Justin's bag from the bench, he began rummaging through it. Not finding what he wanted in the center compartment, he fumbled with the zipper on the outside of the pack.

Justin lunged at the bag. "Give me that." He felt violated.

"Oops." The youth jumped back out of Justin's reach as he stumbled forward. "Bull's eye!" he sneered, holding Justin's wallet in the air just beyond reach.

"Tax time," Leon snickered, stepping between them.

Gino grabbed the wallet from his friend. Pulling the money and credit cards from the inner pockets, he threw the wallet back to its owner.

Justin was dazed. "Can we go now?"

"Not so fast," Gino said, eyeing Ashley.

The shorter one moved in beside him. "I think we should just take your little girlfriend over to the park for a walk first, don't you think so, Gino?"

Leon looked directly at Ashley for the first time. As her hazel eyes flashed momentarily in his direction, he saw his mother's face staring up at him from her bed. They were the same hazel brown eyes. She was stripped to the bone by a ravenous cancer that had attacked in her thirty-seventh year. He could hear her voice telling him to be strong. She had always said he was special. He was seventeen the night she died, lost and alone, rocking her empty, frail body in his arms, begging her to come back.

"Hey little lady, wanna go for a walk?" Gino's voice cut through to present time. He reached for her wrist as he spoke.

Ashley pulled away, frightened.

"Don't be rude, now," he hissed, angrily grabbing her arm.

Justin's face flushed. A blazing anger raged through his body, and his taut fist slammed automatically through the air at Gino.

"No," Leon bellowed and lunged between them to protect his mother as Justin's fist smashed into his jaw. Leon shrieked, staggered, and spun violently backwards, knocking Gino off balance before he slammed to the pavement, dazed.

Leon tasted blood. His hand went up to his face.

Thick red fluid was oozing from his chin. His nostrils flared as he sneered up at Justin. Slowly, deliberately, he turned on his right side and got up. Moving with calculated, methodical steps, all five of them flanked him, surrounding Justin and Ashley in a semicircle.

The ring of five tightened. Leon wiped the blood from his lip and broke into a vicious curse. His voice wild with rage, he screamed obscenities at Justin. The faces of the five seethed as their semicircle closed in around the two.

For an instant Ashley was lost. Was this her dream or the real event? The faces were incensed, uncaring, hard. The taunting circle tightened, and the coarse smell of bodies was overwhelming. She felt as if she was going to throw up. Inhaling sharply, she begged for help. For a split second, time and the scene shifted into slow motion. In that instant her vision altered and she saw through the forms to the light of spirit within. There, hidden beneath the layers of hurt and ugliness in each of the gang members, was a light . . . a jewel.

"My God," she thought, staring up at Leon in awe, "even under all the anger Leon's light is the brightest, nearest to the surface." Ashley's intent turned to steel on the anvil of her heart. She knew he would be the easiest to reach. She had to get to him, even if she didn't know how.

"Leon, stop!" she screamed, jumping to her feet.

It was the first word he had heard out of her mouth, and it stunned him. Leon recoiled. Looking down at her, he reeled back. Her eyes haunted him.

Ashley was praying inwardly for help. She had gotten his attention. Where could she go from here? "Leon, please." Her eyes were wide with fear. Leon stared at her blankly. It was his mother's face he saw, wide-eyed and gaunt, begging him for help.

Ashley sensed his faltering. She'd seen something in him, and it changed her. "Leon . . . ," she repeated, her voice shrill, frightened.

His heart wrenched at the sound. He remembered his mother's agony. Shaking his head, he grimaced in confusion at the plea. He couldn't help her that night or ever again.

Justin looked over at Ashley in startled disbelief. This was the illusive inner strength he'd sensed in her.

"Don't listen to her, Leon." The stocky one grabbed his arm in an attempt to pull him back.

"Leon, there's something special in you," Ashley countered. "I can feel it." She had to reach him. "You're different from the rest."

Leon's face was tortured as he pulled away. He'd heard these words before. His breathing was heavy and labored as he faltered, gaping down at her. His mind was reeling, torn by powerful forces he didn't understand.

"She's just trying to get to you, Leon," Gino bellowed.

Ashley silently prayed for help. She was going on an instinct, but she needed a miracle. She had to separate Leon from the rest to split the group.

"Don't listen Leon," growled the stocky one, jumping forward. His neck was crimson with rage. "Let's take her." He reached over to grab Ashley's wrist.

Abruptly, Leon's arm flew out across his friend's chest. His eyes glazed with an animal torment. "Wait!" he snarled, staring down into Ashley's eyes.

"You're different, Leon," Ashley was begging inwardly for the right words. "You carry a special light," she said finally. "I can see it."

Leon's eyes grew wide with amazement. His body leaned toward her as if drawn by a tremendous force. A strange sensation began churning in his stomach. His mother was the only one who had ever talked to him this way. She had spoken of the light just before she died, said he would discover it one day. He wanted desperately to believe her now.

"Listen to me," Ashley appealed, steadily holding his gaze. "You're a natural leader, Leon."

"Don't be a fool, Leon," Gino barked in his ear. "She's just trying to trick you."

At that very instant there was a noise and a shift in energy at the far end of the street. Leon felt it and looked up. His eyes flinched in terror. For one brief moment Ashley shuddered. Leon looked like a frightened animal cornered for the kill. She felt sorry for him. Following his eyes, Ashley looked up to see seven surly thugs wearing purple arm bands headed in their direction. Leon's gang was outnumbered.

As they approached, one of the boys in the purple gang suddenly caught the drift of what was going on. Pointing, he began a slow, contrived saunter in their direction. His gang fell in step behind him.

"So what have we here?" he jeered at a distance of about twenty feet from them. "Leon's boys are being bad." He stretched out the word "bad" as he mocked the leader of the group.

"And Leon's bleeding," sneered another.

Leon and his gang slowly began stepping back. They moved in a flank, eyeing their rivals as they squared off, facing them at a distance of about ten feet.

Taking advantage of the moment, Justin reached for Ashley's arm and they began edging their way to the street. As soon as they got to the curb, Justin signaled with a squeeze, and they took off in the direction of the Quick Stop store.

Instantly, Elder Em pressed the button and the two began a slow dissolve. The air sizzled and hissed. Startled by the sound, Leon and the others turned and stared in disbelief as the two figures began fading into thin air in the middle of a full running stride. Then Justin and Ashley disappeared completely, and the two gangs were left gaping in their direction in disbelief.

Chapter 11

Reflections

Justin felt as if he was in a time warp as he watched in amazement while Ashley's cells remolecularized in the space beside him. Reaching out to reassure her, he saw his own hands instantly becoming solid as his fingers clasped her arm. Exhausted from the tension, she fell against him, and his arms encircled her shoulders. Élan and Jaron reached the front of the class just as their cells fully reconverged and grabbed the two of them. Each knew what Justin and Ashley had been through. There was no way of duplicating a real experience; experience was the true teacher.

Ashley's knees were weak and her heart still racing. "You're right!" she whispered to Élan as the four embraced. "It's not easy down there."

Jaron stepped back with new respect. "You were great." He wondered if he could have done as well. "I couldn't believe your courage."

"Me too," Justin mumbled, rubbing the dried blood from the cracks in his right hand. It was still numb from the intensity of the blow.

"I agree, Ashley," Brooke added from her fourth-row seat. "Jaron was really courageous, but his situation was easy compared to yours."

Ashley shook her head. "What you saw had nothing to do with courage," she said. "It was sheer survival. We were trapped with no way out." She was humbled. She understood now why no one had a right to judge another. She knew that you could never tell how you would handle a situation until you were in it.

"What Ashley isn't aware of is the gift that she gave Leon." Elder Em walked to the front of the room. "You see, like many of the souls on Earth, Leon was on the edge," he said as he joined the four students beside his desk. "His mother died when he was seventeen," he continued, facing the front of the room now. "Feeling abandoned, he gave up his quest and sought support in other ways. That's what led him to the gang."

"I don't understand." Ashley looked up at the elder quizzically. "What does that have to do with me?"

"The gift that you gave Leon was the gift of recognition," the elder said. "For one moment in time, you saw beyond Leon's facade to who he really is. That moment of insight into Leon's true nature, like the moment that Jaron gave James, will stay with Leon and eventually change his life."

Ashley smiled inwardly. She sensed that somehow she could still see the light in Leon's eyes.

"What about James?" Jaron asked.

"Same thing," the elder answered. "James is going through a change in consciousness even now as we speak."

Jaron wondered what changes James would be going through. After all, he was an old man. How many more years did life hold for him?

"Some day each of you will experience the full measure of your kindness as it comes back to each of you in different forms."

Ashley shivered. Was he alluding to her life to come? She glanced over at Justin, wondering what their separate lives would hold. "But I went in and out of awareness just like Élan said," she said. "How could it be that I gave him a gift?"

"Trust me, you did," the elder said.

"She gave me a gift too," Justin grinned. "If it weren't for Ashley, I wouldn't be here right now!"

"I know, we were watching you," Élan laughed. "I'm sure Ashley's thankful that you volunteered to go down and help her. What would she ever have done without you?" he quipped.

"Don't tease," Ashley intervened.

"Sorry," he acquiesced. Teasing never did feel good to him.

Ashley addressed Justin directly as she spoke. "I did need you, Justin." She couldn't stand seeing him hurt. She had a special place in her heart for him. Ashley looked at Élan. "I was stronger because we were together," she said.

Justin smiled. Even if he didn't believe everything

Ashley was saying, he liked the idea that she defended him. "Can I give my readout on our experience?" he asked.

"Sure," the elder answered.

"Mind if we sit down first?"

"Go ahead Justin." The elder motioned toward the chairs as the four of them sat down.

"I was shocked." Justin shook his head recalling the faces of the gang. "It was an awful experience," he added staring blankly at the wall. "I don't know what I expected on Earth, but I surely didn't expect the violence that we ran into." Justin looked at the elder. "Exclusivity and anger are terrible things, Elder Em." His voice was incredulous. "They stole from us and would have hurt Ashley, all because we were somehow different from them."

Elder Em shook his head. "We have watched this phenomenon for thousands of years, Justin" His eyes were pained, his face filled with empathy. "The absence of love and the separation that it breeds has been the source of suffering on the planet. To this day this condition perpetuates schisms between races, communities, and nations."

Justin was anguished. "But if this condition is so destructive, sir, how could they possibly permit it on Earth? Why would human beings allow it on their planet?"

"It's really easy to live with low-level pain," the elder replied. "People have gotten used to it."

"But I still don't understand." Justin was baffled.

"Why wouldn't they want to create a world without it?"

"Because human beings are not yet aware that life is a creative act, Justin." Elder Em was touched by the depth of Justin's insight. The simulations obviously worked. "People think that life just happens to them. They are the effect of their ego and their emotions. They haven't yet realized that they control their destiny. They haven't seen that they could agree to change the world and that by that agreement the world would indeed begin to change."

"Well, they make it awfully hard on themselves." Justin shook his head reflectively. "They have established a powerful paradigm of fear, hatred, and mistrust. It's really frightening."

Elder Em was at a loss for words. He knew the agony. It was this same anguish that had brought the Planetary Welcoming Committee together some time earlier. He could still hear Raoul's words as he opened the meeting that day. "As beings," he had said, "we are all cells in a great body. When it becomes evident that something in our body is not working, it triggers a deep subconscious pain in the heart of the entire species. My brothers," he had said, "Earth is in need of help."

"This is the reason for the training, Justin," the elder said finally.

"What frightened me the most, Elder Em, was my own reaction to the anger." Justin felt the power of his own rage surging through his body as his fist flew out to find its mark. "I got entangled in the web of energy myself." He felt sick thinking about it.

"Please, Justin, you have to stop beating yourself up," Ashley interjected. "It was only because of me that you got involved."

"You're being kind," he countered weakly.

"No I'm not," Ashley insisted. "You were holding your own, Justin, maintaining real well, until they went after me."

"Believe me, Elder Em," Justin smiled, "she saved me."

"I did not. You were staying quite still until they turned on me. Only then did you lose control."

"You should listen to her, Justin, I think she's right," Elder Em agreed. "Even after you jumped to retrieve your bag, you regained your composure until one of them suggested they take Ashley." He paused. "It takes practice, you know. This thing called being a human being does take time, you know."

"Thanks, Elder Em." Justin was reflective. "I think for the first time I realize how much we really need each other. I thought I was going to help Ashley, and it turned out that she helped me."

"We helped each other," Ashley reminded him.

"But really," Justin said, "it was your diplomacy that turned the tide." He was leaning forward in his chair to look at her two seats away on his right. "You were incredible down there! How did you do it?"

"It wasn't me." Ashley shook her head emphatically. "I was desperate. They had us backed into a corner, Justin. I knew we had nowhere to go." Ashley stopped momentarily, staring up to her left as she mentally reviewed the scene. Then she looked over at Justin again. "It was at that point that I stopped depending on either of us to handle it. I knew we needed help. Without it we were hopeless! Suddenly I got very still and I asked the One for help. I asked from the deepest part of me, Justin." She nodded reflectively. "And I think that's what really did it. It was at that point that I saw the jewel."

"What jewel?" Justin asked in surprise.

"In reflecting back now I can see that is was exactly as the manual said, Justin. The heart has the capacity to see the truth. I suddenly saw beyond the gangs' surface behavior. For one instant, beneath the pretense of their rage, I glimpsed the inner spirit of those guys." Ashley was thoughtful. "I couldn't believe it. I was looking at Leon at the time, and I suddenly saw the jewel of spirit hidden beneath his angry gestures. It was at that point that I got the courage to speak up. I began desperately reaching for him out of an instinctive feeling, praying the whole time for help."

Ashley's eyes lit up. "Then it happened! Miracle of miracles, Leon began to respond, and a turn of events occurred . . . that other gang appeared out of nowhere! Dear God, was I relieved!" She relaxed back into her chair.

"I do have a public admission," she continued. "I

want all of you to know that I inwardly harbored a belief that I might be able to do better than either Élan or Jaron. However, my hidden bravado has been tempered on the anvil of good, hard Earth experience. Élan was right! It's almost impossible to maintain an unbroken state of awareness on the planet. I really tried!"

Elder Em had waited a long time for the teaching to come full circle. Sitting on the edge of his desk, he raised his hands to motion the point. "Ashley has unknowingly hit the crux of the matter," he said. "It is this 'good, hard Earth experience' as she calls it, that usually strengthens the power of resignation, fanning the fire of broken dreams."

Some of the faces were puzzled. He continued slowly. "Over the centuries, millions of people have given up their goals and visions because of it. They have sacrificed hope and individual determination in the face of seemingly overwhelming odds."

More of the students understood now. The confusion was beginning to clear. It showed on their faces. "The key to achieving any goal is to be able to take a stand for that goal in the face of no evidence," he said pausing to consider his alternatives. How could he make the teaching real for them?

"Let me explain," he said. "The great ones on Earth intuitively knew this. They knew that they couldn't depend on the evidence showing up immediately. Let me tell you a story of one of those people." Elder Em paused to accent the beginning of his story.

"Once, there was a man named Gandhi who lived in India during the time of the British rule. Although he was a small and physically unintimidating figure, Gandhi had a great vision for mankind. He once said, 'Man often becomes what he believes . . . if I have the belief that I can do it, I shall surely acquire the capacity to do it even if I may not have it at the beginning.'

"As the young boy grew into a man, he realized that the domination of a people was not right. He dreamed of civil liberty and freedom for his people, and his goal soon crystallized into a plan. His life eventually became his message and the fulfillment of that plan.

"When Gandhi was sixty years of age the British, who were the only legal salt makers in India, tried to levy a salt tax on the Indians. Gandhi realized that the British couldn't maintain the levy without the agreement and cooperation of the Indian people. He decided to walk across India to the sea in protest.

"Seventy-eight people started with him on his two-hundred and fifty mile historic march for civil liberty. His goal was to show his people a nonviolent method of making a difference."

The class was mesmerized. This was the first human Earth story they had ever heard.

"When Gandhi began his march," Elder Em continued, "most of the people were aghast. The English scoffed at him: How could one man really make that much difference?

"So Gandhi began his march with seventy-eight followers. He walked without any physical evidence to support his vision. Inwardly, his faith and courage were strong. He knew he was doing the right thing and, like Ashley, he followed his instinct and asked for help.

"In the twenty-four days that followed, hundreds joined them, and by the time Gandhi reached the sea, his throng was made up of thousands of villagers who joined the march in support of the cause. On the evening of April fifteenth, 1930, Gandhi and his followers reached the coast of India at Dandi Beach. Gandhi spent most of that night in meditative contemplation. At sunrise the next morning, with the eyes of thousands watching him, he rose and walked down into the sea. Then, returning to the shoreline, he bent and picked up some salt that had evaporated from the seawater.

"The result was electrifying. Throughout India salt suddenly became a mysterious word with the power to unite a people. All along the coast, Indians began unlawfully scooping salt.

"Although the salt tax was levied, Gandhi's march restored the Indians' faith in their ability to shape their own reality. Thousands of Indians began using homemade salt. This marked the turning point in Gandhi's lifelong vision of freedom.

"Eventually the method that he taught his people became the model for civil disobedience, and in 1947, some seventeen years after his march, India was restored to freedom. This one man freed his nation from years of bondage because he was willing to take a stand for a dream in the face of no visible evidence."

Élan had tears in his eyes. He knew the challenge. Jaron was stung by the meaning of the story. He was thinking of his last few moments with James. Ashley was openly crying. She had experienced the anguish of standing up to a group in the face of no evidence. Justin was quiet. He felt every word, and so did every other member of the class. Earth was now real. They had been touched by the life of a real man, and their hearts were full. The teaching was now tangible.

Slowly Elder Em went on. "Life will challenge one's commitment," he said. "And only those who continually recommit, striving for the dream in the face of no physical evidence to support it, will finally arrive at the supreme achievement." The elder paused for a long moment. It was almost done. The circle of teaching was almost complete.

Then he added the conclusive stroke. "People need to know their power. If they would be willing to take a stand for a new world, a vision of possibility for their children and their children's children . . . If they would be willing to commit and recommit to this vision, taking small steps toward the goal each day, eventually that new world would come to pass."

Elder Em finished. The room rang with clarity. Every student understood. "Are there any questions?" he asked with finality. He knew there wouldn't be. It was done. The first three simulations and all of their lessons were now complete. A hush had fallen across the room, less in answer to the question than in stillness from the insight. Elder Em moved away from his desk.

"Well, then," he said, "we'll adjourn in preparation for the forth and final simulation. Rest, rejuvenate, and study."

Chapter 12

The Missing Mantra

The texture of Justin's emotions was splotchy at best, raw from his experience, shaken out of his romantic lethargy by his first Earth encounter. "I'm really okay," he insisted in answer to Élan's query. Confused by the mix of emotions, he was standing in his doorway looking out at Élan and Zendar wondering why the two of them had followed him to his room. "Tired though," he added, trying to push back his real feelings.

"Sounds like denial to me." Élan brushed past him. "Can we come in?" he said, entering the room as he spoke. He knew the signs better than that—tension around the edges of Justin's mouth and eyes, a hollow emptiness in his voice. Zendar followed him, scrutinizing Justin's face closely.

"I'll be OK," Justin insisted in answer to Zendar's eyes. "Really."

Élan was uncompromising. "I wanted to be left alone too." He recognized the symptoms all too clearly.

"What do you mean?"

"I was in pretty bad shape after my simulation."

"He actually quit the plan," Zendar asserted flatly.

"Really?" Justin was incredulous; they seemed to know his feelings better than he did.

"Really," Élan confirmed.

"It was far more than that," Zendar continued wryly. "He was a mess. By the time I got to him he was rolled up on the bed vowing that he would never be born."

Justin started to laugh, picturing Élan rolled up on the bed. "Is that really true?" He was staring at Élan. It was hard to imagine his friend having a reaction like that. Élan had always been so certain of his goal.

Élan frowned. "I wasn't quite that bad," he countered. Turning to Zendar he added, "Don't exaggerate, Zen."

"I'm not exaggerating," Zendar laughed, nodding at Justin. "He was awful, totally obnoxious."

"OK. So it was pretty bad," Élan concurred.

Justin laughed openly. His shoulders relaxed. The image of his friend not wanting to be born lightened him up. He could finally share his feelings. "So I'm not the only one feeling confused?"

"Far from it!" Élan answered. "That's why we're here."

Justin inhaled sharply. "So what is it, Élan? Why do I feel so lost?"

"It's the Human Condition, Justin," Élan answered. "It's like a virus. It implants itself in your cells and goes off at a later time. Just when you think you've passed the test, made it through the event, so to speak, resignation sets in." Élan gestured to Zendar. "I'm not sure I could have pulled through without Zen."

Justin nodded, looking over at Zendar. He appreciated their relationship. He knew he needed them now.

"Why don't you come to Élan's room and study with us in case there's some residue." Zendar patted Justin's shoulder.

"You're probably right, the company would be good for me right now." Justin walked over and sat on his bed. He had a plan. He had to take care of something else first. "Tell you what, give me a few minutes to rest, and I'll join you." He stretched out on his bed.

"Promise?"

"Promise."

"It's a deal." Élan gestured in the direction of the door, and Zendar followed. "We'll see you in awhile."

"Soon," Justin confirmed, as the door closed behind them.

With only a moment's hesitation, Justin grabbed his manual and headed for the door. Gingerly opening it, he leaned into the hallway. Discovering that it was empty, he turned left in the direction of Ashley's room.

Scenes flashed rapidly across his mind as he made his way down the hall. *His first morning on Earth and Earth in all her beauty. Ashley and the inner strength he sensed in her that day. How he valued and appreciated her. Her dream. Their bus ride. This confusion over a mistake that wasn't a mistake at all because it led to the fulfillment of her dream. The gang. The fear. The rage when they alluded to taking Ashley . . .*

His heart was flooded with recrimination. *Ashley . . . He had let her down. She would never want to find him when they were born. He couldn't blame her. She was stronger than he was.* His mind raced back through every fear, every emotion. *He regretted the collapse, the loss of personal control. He felt his own anger and rage, his frenzy and the confrontation with his own violence. He flashed back, remembering his awful pleasure as Leon and Gino hit the ground. His shame at his crazed fury in front of Ashley.*

Justin sighed as he whispered Ashley's name beneath his breath. Birth looked dismal without her. After having spent a day with her, how could he ever leave her again? If she would only promise to find him after they were born, then he could relax and enjoy the rest of the training. *Ashley . . . He recalled her sweetness and courage, her sensitivity mixed with an indomitable will, her stillness combined with a greatness of spirit. He regretted hitting a man. He hated losing control. He knew he'd let her down. He had to talk to her.* What if she laughed at him? What would he say to her? He didn't know.

Maybe he could use Élan and Zendar's visit as an intro. That was it. They were concerned about her condition, afraid she might be caught in the Human Condition. But how would he even broach the real question? How would he ever find out her intent?

Reaching her door, he hesitated. His palms were sweaty. Would she think him foolish? No, he must find out if she was OK. It wouldn't be fair not to check on her. After all, both he and Élan had needed help. He began to knock quietly. She opened the door. His heart pounded as their eyes met. She broke the silence. "I've been thinking about you Justin."

"You have?" Justin cleared his throat. "Me too you," he said clumsily. "I came to find out if you're feeling all right."

"Feeling all right?" Ashley's hazel eyes looked puzzled. "What do you mean?"

Justin's voice trembled. "Well, Élan and I . . ." He stared down at her. It was perfectly obvious that she was fine. He suddenly realized that he'd better change the subject. "Never mind," he said. Why did he always feel so awkward in her presence? His heart was still racing. He cleared his throat again and attempted nonchalance. "Uh, you were thinking of me?"

"Well, yes," Ashley smiled. Sometimes Justin seemed so young. She felt as if she could almost read his thoughts. "I . . ." Suddenly she hesitated. She hoped she had read him correctly. "I've been doing a lot of thinking. We were a great team down there. Maybe we should look for each other after we're born?"

Justin's eyes widened. "Great idea," he stammered. "I hadn't thought of it."

"You hadn't?" Ashley sensed his quandary.

"Well I had, sort of," he stuttered awkwardly. He couldn't believe what he was hearing. She wanted to find him too! What a relief. He couldn't have asked for more. Ashley really was committed to finding him. That's all he needed. "Anyway," he pretended nonchalance, "I think you're right."

"Think we can do it?" Ashley asked.

"Do what?" Justin was seeing their meeting. He wondered how old they would be and what they would be wearing.

"Find each other," Ashley repeated.

"I know we can," he said assuredly. He was back now. "I'll find you no matter what, Ashley." He reached for her hand. "I promise."

Ashley nodded. "I'll look for you too." Her eyes were peaceful. Justin felt complete. All the rest was process. They would find each other again someday. He knew it.

Justin squeezed her hand. "Thanks, Ashley." His heart soared. It was done. He turned and began to walk back in the direction he'd come from. Ashley shook her head as she watched him disappear from sight around the corner. What was it about this man? He filled a need in her that even she didn't understand. Was it his youthful innocence or his lack of sophistication about his inner strength? She knew he wasn't fully aware of his ability yet. Someday he would be she vowed, closing the door behind her.

Turning the corner, Justin broke into a run. Arriving at Élan's room, he threw open the door. Jaron and Brooke spun around in the middle of the room where they had been talking to Zendar.

Élan looked up from his window seat in shocked surprise at the shift in Justin's energy. "Is that what a short rest does for you?"

Seeing Jaron and Brooke, Justin hesitated.

"It's OK," Zendar said in answer to Justin's look. "The four of us have gotten pretty close. Come on in."

Justin closed the door behind him. Unable to hide his excitement any longer, he burst out, "She said she'd find me."

"Who said they'd find you?" Élan asked.

"Ashley."

"You went to see Ashley?"

"Just in case of the resignation thing." Justin pulled back. "After you left, I wanted to make sure she was OK."

In the next few minutes Justin shared everything that happened to him after Élan and Zendar had left his room. He spoke of his inner recrimination and shame at the loss of control he'd exhibited in front of Ashley. He spoke of his fear at the anger and rage he had seen in himself that day on Earth. He talked of his feelings for Ashley and the longing to find her after birth. He saw her face at the doorway as he told them what she had said.

Jaron studied his every gesture as he spoke. Enthralled with Justin's candor, he wondered if he could ever be as open and honest about his feelings for Brooke. They had never spoken to each other about the future. Glancing over at her, he wondered what she would say if he dared broach the subject. His hands turned to ice just thinking about it.

When Justin was finished, Jaron heard his own voice excusing the two of them. "Brooke and I have to be going now," he said. She looked at him in shocked surprise, but followed his lead without hesitation.

"I think we'll study on our own this time," she said following him to the door. The depth of Justin's feelings had stirred something in her too.

Justin was instantly contrite as the door closed behind them. "I didn't mean to chase them away." Why had he spilled his emotions in front of them? He should have known better than to talk in front of strangers even if they were Élan and Zendar's friends.

"You didn't." Zendar sat forward on the bed. "I don't think their reaction was about you at all."

"I agree," Élan added. "I think you stirred up something in them that they had never faced."

"Like their feelings for each other." Zendar completed Élan's thoughts. "I don't think Jaron even knew what his true feelings were," he added," until you shared yours."

"Really?" Justin asked.

"It's all conjecture at this point," Zendar shrugged. "But I was watching Jaron's face as you were talking. Something touched him. I could see it in his eyes."

Justin was relieved. Inspired by his conversation with Ashley, he was ready to get on with his studies. "I'm ready to move forward," he said. "Let's study."

Reaching for his manual, Justin turned to the next Mantra and volunteered to read.

• • •

THE MATOS MANTRAS

Believe
(7)

Believe in yourself and believe that all things are possible. The power of the One is infinite. Take a stand for a miracle in the face of no physical evidence. Have faith in life, for life has a way of working out.

Believe that you will receive all that you need to fulfill your destiny and to heal the planet. Life works and it will work through you if you'll just get out of the way and let it.

Surrender
(8)

Surrender to the insight that you are spirit. When we surrender to this insight, the world changes. We can no longer judge or criticize. Nor can we be jealous or hateful.

Surrender your will to the will of the One. Surrender is not giving up. It is not passive. Instead it is taking an active stand to alter the world around us by harnessing the ego with a compassionate heart.

To the soul who surrenders, the heart melts and merges, blending the outer world with the inner. From that moment forth nothing remains the same for this one becomes a carrier of love, giving to others as love has given to him.

"Is that all there is?" Justin turned and looked up at Élan and Zendar from his seat on the floor. "Does your book end where mine does?"

"It seems to," Élan agreed.

"I thought I heard Elder Em say there were nine mantras," Justin said.

"I thought so too," Élan agreed

"Me too!" Zendar affirmed.

"So what happened to the ninth?" Élan kept flipping the pages, half expecting it to appear.

"Mine is blank too," Zendar was staring at the last empty page.

"Maybe they messed up." Justin shrugged. "Think we should talk to Elder Em before he's embarrassed by it in class tomorrow?"

Chapter 13

Rhea's Call

Setting the manual down, Elder Em sat at his desk in the privacy of his own alcove, where the final stages of the plan had been reviewed and completed. Leaning forward on his elbows, he clasped his hands in contemplation. "What a session," he thought as he reviewed the recent series of events.

Justin and Ashley had done very well. He had originally debated on whether or not to send them together, finally choosing to run with the idea in the latter planning phase of the simulation. Now, sitting here at his desk after the fact, he was pleased. The results had been better than he had expected. This particular leg of the simulation had allowed an opportunity for some extensive teaching on the Human Condition

In fact, all in all, the plan was working perfectly. With each new session the students were becoming stronger and more resilient. With each new phase of the simulation their commitment level was rising. Auras were brightening, and with the extensive training, even the amnesia was beginning to lose some of its grip. He had great hopes for the next phase. The more his students could counter the effect of the amnesia during the simulation, the greater their chances of success after they were born. This would accelerate their awakenings from the amnesia on Earth. All in all it would move the Earth closer to its moment of critical mass.

Elder Em stretched back in his swivel chair with a sigh of satisfaction. The session had been full and rich, and now there was the aftermath of tiredness. Intending a momentary nap to rejuvenate himself, he leaned back into the cushioned chair. As he did, he slipped beneath the landscape of consciousness into the world of dreams where events transpire in a different continuum.

Translucent images overlapped and dissolved into one another. His breathing deepened as he plummeted into a timeless terrain of flashing scenes: *The Earth with its searing distortion and its plea for help. The original proposal and the final training plan. Raoul's face and the look they exchanged as the first manual was completed.*

Then pictures of the training ripped by sporadically: *Élan's face as he walked to the front of the room to be the first participant in the simulation; Jaron as he fought the sadness in the boat with James; Justin and Ashley receiving their final instructions before leaving; the couple surrounded by hateful taunting faces; Élan alone in the swirling water at the river's edge; Zendar's body standing rigid as he watched his friend caught in the river's current; Brooke's eyes as she followed every move that Jaron made in his simulation; Élan and Zendar as*

Élan remolecularized in the front of the room; and Élan's candid question about Rhea.

Suddenly the scene changed. Elder Em found himself standing in a field of yellow flowers. To the east was Mount Akros. To the west was a small solitary figure walking along a path in the direction of the mountain. At first he couldn't make out the form. Then he saw that it was a woman. Even at a distance he could feel her energy . . . it was Rhea. She walked with a sense of purpose, as if she was on a journey and knew her destination. As she approached, Elder Em caught a glimpse of her face. It was radiant. She was lighthearted and happy, yet focused and intent. He watched her for some time and she never looked up or noticed. She appeared to be deeply resolute.

Suddenly Elder Em had a strange, icy feeling. It came up from his feet, swallowing his knees and thighs as it spread throughout his body. Looking down he stared in horror as one by one the entire hill of brightly colored flowers turned to brown and withered before his eyes. Like a picture postcard that had faded in the sun, the entire scene turned a muddy color. He turned to walk, but his feet were heavy. Death was everywhere he looked. His every step became slow and labored.

Elder Em moaned and turned his head slightly to the right as the scene shifted again. He was suddenly in a city, walking quickly down a long street. He was searching for Rhea. He sensed she was lost, deep in despair, overcome with grief. Every corner he turned led to a dead end. He called her name, and it echoed from the building walls.

Then the streets disappeared and Rhea was standing directly in front of him in the middle of a large room. Wearing a blue suit, she looked suddenly small, dwarfed by the size of the room. Her features were hollow. Her eyes were pleading, round, and wistful, strained around the edges. "I need your help," she said simply, quietly. "I've lost my way."

As his hand went out to reach for her, a knock at the door sharply broke the contact. The scene slipped away from his grasp. Elder Em sat bolt upright, and Rhea vanished beyond the border of his mind. "Where is she?" he thought, blinking back the torment and the pain.

Realizing that someone was at the door, he tried to compose himself. "Come in," he called half-consciously. The door swung open on the right hand of Justin. Élan was standing in the hall just behind.

"Well." The elder inhaled sharply, quickly feigning buoyancy. "What are you two doing here?" Still trying to regain his equilibrium, he added, "And where's Zendar?" It was Rhea's face he saw as he spoke. He could still feel the icy chill as the color of death flashed through his body. The dream had left him with an awful foreboding.

"He wanted to review the text once more before class," Justin answered.

"Please," the elder faltered slightly in an attempt

at composure, "come on in."He shook his head trying to collect himself. It was Rhea's face he saw as he spoke.

"Did we interrupt?" Élan couldn't help but notice the look on the elder's face.

"Not really. Just caught me cat-napping!" Seeing the confusion in their faces at the phrase, he added quickly, "Sorry, it's an Earth saying for a small nap. I'm still a bit between worlds!" he added, standing to greet the young men as they entered. "Come on in."

He pointed down the length of the room. "Let's move into the other section," he said. "It's far more comfortable."

The two followed him into the sleeping chamber of his extended rooms. Élan immediately noticed its size. It was large enough to include a full sitting area. The bed was against the far wall next to the door and immediately in front of him was a couch and two matching chairs forming a semicircle. A long, low table was in the center of the chairs. Elder Em walked over to the corner lamp and turned a small dial beneath the shade.

He gestured to a seat on the couch, choosing one of the chairs himself. "How may I help you?

"This is just a quick visit," Justin said uncomfortably. He was sorry now that he'd insisted on coming. Why hadn't he listened to the signals. Both Élan and Zendar had wanted to talk to the elder in class. Under duress Élan had finally agreed to accompany him. "It's about the manual," he said awkwardly, holding up his book as he spoke.

"Yes." Elder Em sensed what was coming. It had to be the missing mantra. He had anticipated this, but not so quickly. He had expected to handle the question back in the class. He never suspected any of his students might come to visit him privately about it. But Justin was so impetuous, he should have known. Caught off guard, he wasn't sure what to say. He had counted on the classroom setting to help him handle it.

"Well, the three of us were studying together and we noticed that a page was dropped out." Justin fumbled ahead, unable to back out now.

"What do you mean a page dropped out?

"I don't know sir," he hesitated.

"Didn't you say that there were nine mantras?" Élan jumped in to ease Justin's embarrassment.

"Yes."

"Well, then," Justin added, feeling Élan's support, "the ninth one must be missing." He flipped the pages until he got to the eighth mantra. "Look," he said turning one more page as he spoke, "it's only the appendix. Where's the ninth? The last page is blank."

"Don't tell me it slipped by our inspection," Elder Em said as he reached over and took the book from Justin's hand. "You're right, it appears a page is missing.

This was perfect, these two were giving him the perfect alibi. "We checked the book ourselves," he said. "How could a mistake slip by? I'll make sure that we discuss it during the next session, all right?

"Great, Elder Em. Well I guess that's it." Justin, still a bit ill at ease in the elder's presence, signaled Élan with his eyes, and the two stood to excuse themselves. "We just wanted to warn you before class so you weren't taken by surprise."

"Thanks, Justin, I really appreciate that." Elder Em walked the two to the door. Then, spotting an opportunity, he turned to Élan. "Do you mind staying back for a moment?" Élan was startled. He had wanted to talk with the elder too.

"OK with you, Justin?" Élan asked.

"Sure," Justin answered, relieved that he wasn't the one the elder wanted to talk to. Realizing that he had made a mistake in timing, he had felt awkward during the entire visit.

"Thanks for coming by." Elder Em patted Justin's shoulder as he opened the door for him.

"See you soon." Justin nodded at the two of them. "Back in class," he added as he started down the hall.

"Is it Rhea?" Élan blurted out as the door closed, leaving the two of them alone in the room. She was always foremost in his mind, and he hoped the elder had some news of her.

"Well, sort of." The elder's eyes shot a startled look

his way. "But only in a roundabout way." He turned into the room, gesturing to the chairs. "It's really about you. How are you doing, Élan?"

"Me?" Élan was surprised. "I'm doing fine, Elder Em." And then thinking that he might be referring to the backlash, he added, "I had a little setback after the first simulation, but I've come out of it and I'm doing really well now."

Elder Em seated himself and signaled for Élan to do the same. His eyes searched the young man's face. He wasn't exactly sure what he wanted to say or where to start. He had moved on impulse. Something about the dream had left him edgy. He knew he needed to help Rhea, but he wasn't sure what that meant or what it would require. He needed to talk with Élan to ascertain his strength. "I'm not quite sure where to begin, Élan. I'm moving on a feeling, so forgive me if I appear clumsy."

"It's all right." Élan sensed the elder's torment. "Tell me what's on your mind and I'll try to understand."

The elder stood. Images of Rhea tugged at him as he moved toward the window in his room. Pulling the curtain aside, he gazed into the thick fog beyond. Élan momentarily wondered if Elder Em had ever penetrated the mist. If he had almost done it, then surely the elder must have been able to pierce the ethers to view the other side.

"I've wanted to speak with you for awhile, but the timing hasn't been right." The elder's words slipped between Élan's thoughts. "Have you studied the last two mantras?"

"I studied the last two that we received. Nine was missing." Élan leaned forward, curious. "Why?"

"Those are the two I meant." The elder turned from the window. "Because those two will have a special meaning for you someday."

"How's that?" Élan sensed that he was trying to say something more.

"Birth is coming soon." Élan nodded. "And in your lifetime, in your work, Élan, you'll need to believe in yourself." The elder walked over to the couch and seated himself. His long gray robe fell in folds around his feet. "Like many souls this time around, your life will be a challenging one. You'll be pulled in many directions, but there will be a path, a way for you. In order to follow it you will need to go within and believe in yourself and your own inner connection. Do you understand?"

"I think so, Elder Em." Élan was thoughtful. "I think that I believe in myself enough to follow my own heart. That's kind of like listening to the song of my own soul."

"Listening and belief are definitely connected."

"But I'm not sure I understand how surrender fits in all of this."

"How do you think it fits?"

Élan's eyes scanned the floor. "Surrender is one of the deeper concepts. I think it encompasses a myriad of things." Élan stood and moved away from the sitting area. Pacing, he gathered his thoughts. "Zendar, Justin, and I really wrestled with this one." He gazed into the fog at the window and then turned back to face the elder. "Surrender seems to be a paradox. Justin thought it meant that he and Ashley should have surrendered to the gang. But we finally decided that that wasn't it. Surrender isn't quitting and it's not giving up." He paused. "I think surrender is a conscious choice. It is an active decision to accept and work with things the way they are."

"That's good." The elder was pleased with the depth of his insight, but it was still philosophical. "Anchor that in reality for me, Élan."

"That's where I flounder, Elder Em." Élan shook his head. "My Earth experience is limited, so a lot of times I have trouble giving tangible examples. Can you help me."

"Let's use your life as an example."

"You mean the life that's coming for me?"

"Yes." The elder leaned forward in his chair. He was thinking of Rhea. "You may not always get what you think you want in life, Élan, but that's where surrender comes in."

Élan sat down, puzzled. "I'm not sure I understand, but go on."

"At times you may ask for something and it may seem that you're not getting it. You may feel very lost or alone in life. But it's at those very times that surrender comes in. You see, a greater wisdom directs our lives and cares for each and every one of us. You will have to believe that this greater wisdom holds the whole in place and moves life forward. You will have to surrender the small window of your awareness to the greater vision of the all and trust that this wondrous web of consciousness will lead you to your heart's true love in a more miraculous way than even you could have thought possible."

"Are you speaking of Rhea?"

"I am. And of other things also."

"Such as . . ."

"The job that you are going to do."

"Will it be a struggle then?"

"At times."

"Will it ever bring me joy?"

"Great joy. But it won't come quickly. It will unfold in its own time."

"My head is puzzled. But my heart feels and understands." Élan was still. He heard the silent melody he'd heard on Earth when he faced the mountain. It was his own song. "Thank you, Elder Em. I love you."

"I love you too, my son."

"Is that all?"

"Yes." He answered quietly. "It's done."

As the elder walked his student to the door, both felt the bond. Élan knew that this moment would somehow stay with him and sustain him in time of need.

As he closed the door behind him, Elder Em was immediately pensive. He walked slowly through his living area back toward his study. The plan was falling into place. Élan was set. He had been forewarned and strengthened. Zendar was in preparation. Jaron and Brooke were beginning to understand that there was more to their relationship than they originally thought. Justin and Ashley were discovering their commitment. The power of their love would eventually sustain others in the plan.

Now there was Rhea. Thoughts of her pulled him back to the dream. Gazing at his desk, he could almost recreate every scene. He saw her eyes, wide with pleading, strained. Her voice echoed across his mind: "I need your help. I've lost my way."

He felt her emptiness, her despair. What had happened? What had gone wrong. Had he been too immersed in this new training program? The last he knew she had been teaching school under Tara's guidance. He truly believed she was fine, stable in her journey. What had occurred since then? Something must have changed.

Sitting down at his desk, he bowed his head in thought. As he did he stilled his mind, asking for an answer. Soundless thunder swallowed him until all awareness of the space around him fell away. He waited with a pure intention and suddenly it came. His mind was set, a daring new option had been shown.

Chapter 14

The Last Simulation

Zendar was ready. He'd counseled with his friends through the aftermath of three simulations. He'd seen the resultant effect of Earth's energies and the Human Condition on their individual psyches. He'd thought a lot about it and he felt prepared, at least as prepared as he'd ever be. He wasn't naive. He wasn't foolish enough to think himself exempt or above it all. But he knew he'd done his best, and that, after all, was all a person could do.

Elder Em noticed him as he entered the room a step behind Élan. His attention seemed focused on some deep inner flame. Zendar didn't notice the elder's eyes following him as he moved to his chair. He sat with the certainty of a quiet intent, but without any sense of pretense. He was completely preoccupied, his mind engaged in an objective. Zendar was praying for strength and good fortune, two things that every person needs for the quest.

Élan was alert to the unspoken message in Zendar's silence. Élan knew that this was Zendar's time. He felt it in every cell of his body. Élan would have chosen to be with him, but he knew from his own experience that each one goes out alone. Observing his friend out of the corner of his eye, Élan implored the great divine for his protection. Zendar was the best of the best, and he deserved the support of heaven.

Élan looked up just as Justin entered the room. His gait was light and his spirits seemed high. He signaled a quiet "thank you" to Élan as he sat next to Ashley on the far side of the room. Élan signaled back and nodded a smile. He appreciated Justin. He felt a special bond between them now.

A moment later Brooke entered the room with Jaron holding the door behind her. Élan signaled to Zendar. The two seemed content as they seated themselves next to each other in the back of the room. For a moment he was almost envious. Thinking of his recent conversation with the elder, he knew his path would be different. It would require a different kind of fortitude.

Shifting his awareness to the larger field around him, Élan noticed a hushed excitement in the air. A kind of expectancy hung like a premonition in the atmosphere today. It was the final simulation. Something special seemed to be waiting behind the veil of these last few moments. An event was about to happen. "It's in the air," Élan thought. Everyone else seemed to sense it too. All around students were whispering to each other. Élan wondered if it was the mystery of the missing mantra, or if it was the exhilaration of the last venture. "Probably both," he thought.

He shivered as Elder Em stepped to the front of the room. There was something momentous in the occasion of his movement. "The final simulation is about to begin," the Elder announced. His hands went up in a gesture of silence. "I know that many of you have come with questions, and I promise that all of these will be answered during this final phase of our learning."

Justin's hand relaxed. He had intended to open with the question of the mantra, but Elder Em was asking him to wait.

"I am asking you to trust the process," he continued as he slowly caught Justin's eye. "Now is the time to believe and surrender. Believe in your preparation and your ability, and surrender to the process and the path. Each of you is special," he continued, "and as we begin this final simulation, each of you will live in the heart and mind of the individual who volunteers." He paused. "This final simulation is the most challenging in that it represents the apex of our work together."

"Then I'm ready," Zendar said quietly, standing in the center of the room. A hush fell in the room. Zendar's presence was noticeable. Élan watched his friend as he moved to the front of the class, regal and sure in his stride.

The elder smiled as Zendar approached him. He too was proud of Zendar's development. "This is the final leg of our journey," he said to the young man who was standing before him now. "You will be landing in Madison, a bustling city of more than seven million people."

As the Elder talked, Zendar was instantly clothed in Earth attire. "The city is approximately seventy-five miles from the base of Mount Akros. Your identification is already in your pocket."

Zendar reached back in surprise. His pocket was bulky. He smiled. "You're unbelievable, Elder Em!" The tension relaxed in the room.

"In this final simulation, Zendar, you will face the Sirens of Success. These three sorcerers seek to captivate everyone. People have lost their sense of real values, for the sirens of power, fame, and money vie for their attention."

Elder Em looked up at the room as he continued. "These sirens make their home everywhere on the planet, but they really thrive in all the cities of the world. They are a dangerous threesome, for one of the three almost always imprisons people." Elder Em paused and looked at Zendar now. "The two you will deal with are money and prestige as an aspect of fame. Any questions, Zendar?"

Zendar nodded in the negative. "Not right now, sir," he said. "But I'm sure I will later!"

"The keys to your success are belief and surrender, Zendar." The elder looked him steadily in the eye. "Believe in yourself and your ability, while surrendering to the all."

"Isn't that paradoxical, sir?" Zendar asked.

"Life on Earth *is* paradoxical, Zendar. You will find that right action often lies somewhere between two seeming polarities, and usually includes the two."

Élan was watching the interaction between student and teacher closely. Their eyes were locked in an exchange that alluded to deeper meanings.

"Balance strength with suppleness, and you will find your way," the elder concluded as he stood back from his pupil.

"Thank you, Elder Em. I've prayed to be able to do that," Zendar whispered as he turned to face the class.

Élan sat back in his seat. "This is it," he thought. "You go, Zendar. Do well my friend!"

Elder Em stepped behind his desk and pressed the button on the wall. The front of the room sizzled with intensity, and Zendar dissolved before their eyes.

Instantly, the scene ignited. Sounds of freeways and city streets filled the course room. A police siren screamed in the background and then faded out of earshot. Zendar had landed in the downtown metropolis of Madison, remolecularizing in the midst of dozens of pedestrians on a street corner waiting for the light to change. A few of the people next to him noticed something strange as he converged before their very eyes. But before they could figure it out, the light changed, and a massive surge of bodies pressed forward, forcing their attention in the direction of the flow.

Carried along by the momentum, Zendar was unaware that the movement of the crowd had saved him from creating havoc in the city streets. As the mob propelled him forward, he experienced feelings foreign to him. First, there was the external rush of bodies and energies. Then, the sounds of the city streets: voices and cars mixed into a combination of discordant afternoon sounds.

Zendar was relieved as the crowd ebbed onto the sidewalk and began to disperse in various directions. Once he had his bearings, he began to edge his way toward the side of a building where he positioned himself with his back against a store window. This allowed the river of bodies to flow past him. Never had he seen so many people moving so rapidly walking in so many different directions at once. Strange feelings of apathy floated through him as he stood watching the crowd surge according to a system of changing lights. Never had he felt so small and meaningless.

As Zendar gazed into the crowd, he wondered where he was. Even though there were people all around, he felt lost and empty. These sensations of emptiness were strangely familiar, but the source of their familiarity eluded him now. The pulsing cacophony of the city at rush hour and the crush of the surging throng filled his senses as he gazed through the crowd to the city street beyond. Why the energy? Why the bustle? Meanings escaped him.

Minutes passed and Zendar was still staring

through the swarm of people from his vantage point flat against the window. The crowd was beginning to feather out now, but the sounds of horns and traffic on the streets was still at peak intensity. Not understanding the ebb and flow of rush-hour business, Zendar assumed the surge of traffic to be continuous.

"I've got to get my bearings," he thought.

Looking to the left and right for a way of retreat, he immediately spotted a door about thirty feet away. Edging his way into the thinning flow of people, he moved toward it. The sign on the door instructed him to push, and as he did, he found himself standing in a large room with vaulted ceilings. Everywhere he looked there were glass counters, and directly in front of him at a distance of about twenty feet away was a circular wooden encasement with a woman standing in it. The sign on the counter in front of her read INFORMATION.

"Exactly what I need!" he thought, walking over to the counter.

"Excuse me," he said to the woman on the other side. "I'm in need of some information about where I am."

"Of course," she smiled. She was wearing a simple yet elegant teal jacket. As she placed her hand on the counter, Zendar noticed that her nails were a soft mauve color.

"I'm a bit turned around," he said, wondering momentarily about colored nails. He'd never seen anything like them before. "Can you tell me where I am?"

"Why yes!" Her smile was friendly and there was a self-possessed confidence about her. Zendar felt immediately welcomed. Reaching below the countertop, she pulled out a turquoise and green map. Unfolding it in front of him, she asked, "Have you been to Daltons before?"

"Daltons?" Zendar queried. "Is that the name of this town?"

"Oh I see," she laughed, amused. He was such a striking young man, tall and self-contained, with such deep blue eyes. She had failed to recognize the naiveté behind the handsome exterior. She should have noticed it. All the country people had that same "youthful innocence" when they came to town. "You must be new in the vicinity."

"You're right, this is my first time in the area."

"Well, let me settle your mind! The name of the city is Madison. The store is Daltons." She paused and then added enthusiastically, "You're going to love it here."

"I'm sure I am," he said politely.

Watching him closely, she pursued, "I remember my first visit to Daltons. I fell in love with it. In fact, I got so carried away that I spent hundreds of dollars before I realized what I was doing."

Zendar was puzzled by the comment, but he went along with her. She was, after all, a very pleasant person.

"Look here," she said, focusing his attention on the map, "this is where you're standing" She pointed to an X on the green region of the map. "Right here!"

"The men's and boys' departments are over here." Her finger moved across the map as she spoke. "And the electronics department is on the fourth floor; it's a favorite of all the men I know!"

"This all sounds very exciting." Zendar was confused, but he didn't want to be rude. He had expected a map of the city. He felt she was trying to be helpful, but he was lost and a map of the store wouldn't help. "Thank you for your kindness." A lot of things felt strange. What was her fascination with shopping? He was puzzled by her excitement with the store.

"This is my first trip to town and I'm looking for a place to spend the night. Maybe tomorrow I can get back here with enough time to really enjoy Daltons."

"Oh, I understand. You're probably exhausted from your trip."

"I really am," Zendar assented, relieved that she'd found an excuse for him.

"Well, I know a place for you. It's a quiet little hotel about seven blocks from here. It's not too expensive," she said, reaching below the counter for a piece of paper and a pencil, "and you'll be able to get back here easily in the morning on our free shuttle."

"Exactly what I need," he said referring to both. "Thank you."

As Zendar watched, she began to draw a simplified map showing the streets and cross streets in the area. "It's kind of a quaint little place built in the early eighties. It's been nicely kept, so it's clean and neat and close to the downtown area." She stood back, holding her drawing in the air for a moment, gauging her perspective as she talked. Deciding something was missing, she placed the map on the counter and began drawing again.

"What about a place to get something to eat?" he asked. "Is there something in the area?"

"How do you like Italian food?"

"Love it." Zendar hoped he did.

"Then I know the perfect spot right along the way to your hotel. Here," she said, pointing with her pencil to a spot on the now completed map. "It's a cute little place called Adrienne's. They serve good Italian food in a homey setting," she said. "You can't miss it. Just turn on this street," she added, leaning over the counter and motioning in the direction of the street they were on.

"It's about five blocks over from here. It's cuisine on a family budget!" Writing the name of the restaurant on the map she'd drawn, she marked the exact location with a small X.

"Can I help you with anything else?" she asked, handing him the piece of paper.

"That's it," he answered. "Thanks so much." Folding the map, he moved toward the door. Zendar found the sidewalks fairly empty now. It was the edge of twilight, and the sounds of evening traffic were replacing those of day. Unfolding his map, he set out in the direction that the woman had suggested.

Zendar relaxed into the shades of evening. Orange and violet tinted the building walls high above his head, and he slowed to a stroll, captivated by the twilight colors. He drifted in the direction the map specified, stopping now and then to look into the department store windows. One by one they came alive with the neon lights. Without the crush of people and traffic, he found himself attracted to the window displays and the evening sounds of the city streets. It was a pleasant summer night, and warm summer gusts caught his hair as he walked.

In this languid manner city blocks fell away beneath his feet. Before he knew it, Zendar had turned the corner onto the street of the restaurant. The woman at the information booth was right. You couldn't miss it. A bold blue neon sign hung on the wall of the old red brick structure announcing, *Adrienne's—The Best Italian Food in Town.*

"All right," he thought. "I'm starving!"

Zendar opened the squeaky wooden door and entered a quaint, softly lit room. It was filled with wooden tables covered with crisp white tablecloths. Each table contained a small round candle in the center, and the flickering effect cast a subtle aura in the room. The walls were of roughly hewn wood, bare except for a single large lithograph of the old Italian masters on each one. An Italian aria was playing quietly in the background. The entire effect was a feeling of old Italy, except for the standing wooden sign just inside the door that read, "Please Wait for Hostess to Seat You."

The aroma of homemade soup and garlic bread reached him as he waited for the hostess. Zendar felt peaceful. All felt well in the world as the hostess seated him at a corner table, smiled, and handed him a menu.

Zendar was lost in thought, staring down at the menu when she entered. She was a striking woman of average height. She quietly placed her briefcase on the empty chair beside her as she sat at the corner table facing the window. She was wearing a powder blue silk suit, and her dark brown hair touched the collar's edge on her white blouse.

In the course room Élan was pulled out of his seat by the magnetism of her aura. The energy was undeniable. Recognition spread through his entire body. "Rhea," he whispered. "Oh my God, it's you . . ." Standing beside his chair, Élan's eyes filled and softly overflowed, tears spilling down his cheeks. His heart ached. How long had he waited, peering out of the window longing for just one glimpse of her? And here she was now standing before him. "What a striking woman," he thought. And then he wondered. There was a mood of emptiness around her. It was the same feeling he felt after his simulation.

"You've got to see her, Zendar," he murmured. "Zendar, you must sense her, please look up."

At that moment Zendar lifted his head out of the menu and looked around. Something felt different, like a tone or a feeling that he once knew. A strange familiarity was in the air. He looked to the left, but his face felt cold. He turned to the right and a warmth flushed through him as his eyes fell on the woman in blue sitting at a corner table across the room. She looked weary from a day's work in the city.

Zendar's head was spinning. "What is it?" he thought. Something about her tugged at him, but, still, she was a complete stranger. "I can't just walk up to her," he argued under his breath.

"Oh yes you can," Élan whispered. So this is what the elder meant. He must reach his friend.

"This isn't an accident, Zendar." Élan's knees were weak, his throat parched. He had to surrender to the course of events. "It has to be part of the plan, Zendar. Now get up."

"That's crazy," Zendar said. "I can't just walk over to her and start a conversation."

"If I can handle it, you can too." Élan was adamant. "This is an opportunity that won't come again. Now get out of your seat and go over to her."

Zendar stood up and began moving in Rhea's direction as if in a trance. "What will I ever say to her," he thought.

"Just say hello," Élan said. "Hi, my name is Zendar."

Zendar walked over to her side. "Hello," he said. "My name is Zendar." The young woman stared up at him in startled disbelief. "And I don't know why I'm doing this," he added anxiously.

"I don't know why you are either." Her voice was caustic.

"I've never done anything like this before." Zendar insisted. His palms were wet, clammy. His voice was shaky. He wondered why he was doing this. She was obviously put out about it.

"Then why are you doing it now?" she said sarcastically. "His eyes," she thought. They seemed to see right through her.

But it wasn't his blue eyes or his finely chiseled features. It was nothing physical, this sense of affinity. It came from somewhere else. What was happening? She never spoke to men she didn't know. Her heart was pounding. What did he want? "Oh, dear God," she thought. "This man is so familiar." Life seemed to skip a beat as a shiver went through her body.

"Rhea." Élan's love dissolved the distance between them. "Don't turn away from him. It's ordained. Answer destiny's call."

"I'm sorry," she said, attempting composure. "I missed your name." Why did she feel drawn?

"Zendar," he stammered, shaken by her attitude. "It's Zendar." His eyes were pleading, tender. "May I sit down?"

"I don't know," she hesitated. This was ridiculous. "What do you want?"

"I just want to talk to you for a minute."

She was wary, but what harm could it do? After all they were in a public place. "But this is crazy," she thought. "It goes against everything I know."

"Please." Zendar was persuasive. "Just for a minute."

"Well," she said, still indecisive, "just for a minute." She lifted her briefcase off the seat to make room for him and placed it on the floor.

"Thank you," Zendar said, pulling the chair away from the table and seating himself. He felt awkward. "What's your name?" he asked trying to assuage his discomfort.

"My name is Rhea," she answered. "And I don't usually talk to strangers." Actually, she didn't ever talk to strangers. She was a very private person. This was totally out of character for her.

"Neither do I," Zendar replied, staring at her. She was so familiar. Maybe it was her eyes, a deep brown that sparkled with anticipation. There was a depth to her, he could tell. "But I feel as if I know you."

Rhea's mind went to make a cryptic comment, but it couldn't. There was something about him that was so disarming. He was a gentleman in the truest sense of the word. She could feel it. Without knowing why, she trusted him. She smiled slightly in acceptance.

"I don't know where to begin." Zendar folded his hands on the table in front of him.

"Just jump in, Zendar," Élan said. "Tell her about your quest, and the mountain, and the goal."

"I guess I should just jump in," Zendar said. "I'm new in town, and I need to get to Mount Akros."

"Mount Akros?" So that was it! She should have known. Of course he wasn't like the rest of the men in her life. He was on a quest. He had gotten her attention.

"I heard there's a cave there," he said. "And I need to find it."

"Some say it's just a rumor," she said, testing him.

"Others say that's a smoke screen to keep the false seekers away."

"So you know the goal?" Her shoulders dropped and she sank back in her chair. No wonder he was different. She was suddenly sad.

"What is it?" He didn't understand her sudden change of mood.

"My whole life just flashed before me." She was gazing into the street light beyond the window.

"How's that?"

"I was seeking the cave once myself." She appeared reconciled. "But not any more," she shrugged. "Life in the city gets to you after awhile."

"What do you mean?"

"I mean that I've given up the quest."

"You've given up the quest?" Zendar was stymied. "How could anyone give up the quest for the cave?"

"Some do I guess. I did."

"I don't understand," he was visibly shaken. "What happened?"

"It's a long story, Zendar."

"Well I want to hear it."

"What for?"

"Because I'm interested."

"In what?"

"In you and in the quest. I don't understand how anyone could give it up."

"It doesn't matter."

"Yes it does." Zendar was insistent. Rhea searched his face. Who was this man? Moments ago he was a perfect stranger. Why was he barging in on her this way? Why did she feel compelled to answer?

"Well, if it's that important to you," she acquiesced.

"It is."

"Where do I begin?" Her eyes examined the tablecloth as if to find an answer there.

"I used to teach, Zendar. I was a seventh-grade teacher." She paused, reflecting on her past. "It was my love, my great joy in life. My children were everything to me. I worked hard to reach them, and in time they responded." Rhea twisted her napkin and peered blankly through the window to the darkened street beyond. She was somber now.

"Then I met a man, a wonderful man who shared my dreams. His name was Marc. We fell in love and planned to marry."

"Sounds wonderful, what happened?"

"At the time I lived in St. Claire, about a hundred and fifty miles from here. He lived here in the city. For awhile we had a weekend romance. Either he would come to St. Claire or I would drive to Madison. After he proposed, we knew we had to make a decision about our living situation. He couldn't afford to leave his job because of the money, so I gave up my job and moved to the city. I hoped to find another teaching position once we married and settled in." Rhea blinked to choke back the emotion.

"Marc was killed in a car accident just months before the wedding."

"I'm sorry," Zendar whispered. He could feel her pain.

" It was a freak accident," she went on. "A trailer veered out of control and slammed across the highway, careening into his car. Death was instantaneous." She was staring blankly at her hands clasped tightly on the table in front of her. "As you can imagine, with such a sudden death I went into a state of shock." Tears welled up in Zendar's eyes as he listened.

"At first, I denied it," she continued. "I was totally devastated. My plans and dreams had been cruelly ripped from me. I didn't know what to do or where to turn. Life looked meaningless. Nothing mattered.

"Time passed. Finally, when my money ran out, I had to admit the truth: I was alone with nothing to fill the enormous void. Two things were pressing, the need for money and the need to pull myself out of the despair over my loss. It didn't happen quickly. The money came more easily. I couldn't go back to my old job because the position was filled. And, it was too late in the year to obtain a teaching job in the city, but my teaching credentials and finance background landed me a position in an investment agency. The money was extremely good, at least double that of my former salary, and for awhile it really helped to fill the emptiness."

Zendar listened intently. The light from the street lamps outside the window cast a gentle glow across Rhea's face. Her eyes were moist with concealed tears. Why did he feel her pain so intensely? He couldn't take his eyes off her as she began to speak again.

"A lot of other things happened after that." She heaved a deep sigh. "But none of it really mattered. Marc was gone and I had to put my life together as best I could." Rhea stopped, suddenly aware of her surroundings. "Forgive me," she said. "I got carried away. I don't even know you."

Zendar's voice was soothing. "I needed to hear your story, Rhea. But I'm still puzzled. I don't understand why you've given up the quest."

Just then the waitress walked up and placed two glasses of water on the table. "I'm so sorry I didn't get to you sooner," she said, insensitive to the disturbance. "What can I get for you?"

Rhea looked up, jarred by the untimely interruption. "Just a lemon-lime for me. What about you, Zendar?" She wasn't really hungry anymore.

"Same," he said.

"Anything else?" She scribbled the order hurriedly on a ticket.

"Later, maybe," Zendar said, gesturing toward Rhea. "Old friends. We just need to talk."

"OK, I'll get your drinks." Any other night it probably would have bothered her, people coming in at dinner hour just wanting to talk. But tonight it was busy and she was handling the floor alone.

"Where were we?" Rhea took a sip of water.

"You just said you didn't know me and life interrupted you." Zendar smiled. "Life is like that, you know!"

"How's that?"

"Well, we're kindred spirits. You're supposed to be sharing with me. Zendar looked into her eyes. "Trust me," he said earnestly. "We should be sharing with one another."

The waitress leaned over Rhea's shoulder and placed the two drinks on the table. "Anything else?"

"Not right now, thanks," Zendar said. "Go on," he said, turning back to Rhea. His sincerity was convincing.

"Well, there isn't much more," Rhea shrugged. "I learned the ropes of the business fairly easily and began moving up the ladder quickly. All of this started to fill the vacuum. Suddenly I had people around. They looked up to me and I was needed." She looked pensive. "Of course, it couldn't take Marc's place. But time does help, and eventually I began a long and arduous healing process. I'm now working as much as twelve to fourteen hours a day. It fills the void, and more. I've got a beautiful home. The work benefits are good and the bonuses are excellent, allowing me elaborate vacations. I control my own life, Zendar. If I can't have Marc, what more is there? At least I'm secure."

She turned her glass slowly in her right hand, staring unconsciously at the beads of water forming on her fingers. "I believed in the journey once," she said dully. "But I don't have the enthusiasm or zest for life that I used to have, and I'm no longer naive. I'm tired, Zendar. I've aged decades in the last year and a half. Something in me died when Marc died."

Zendar was quiet. He finally understood. She was addicted. Rhea had replaced her need for Marc with the need for work. Now, working long hours, she had truly lost her way. Work and prestige had consumed her. "So the cave became a distant dream?" he asked.

"Well, I hadn't thought of it since Marc's death—not until this very conversation."

She shook her head as if to dispel old images and

dreams of another time. "I used to speak to my students about purpose a long time ago. But now, it seems, I've lost mine." Her voice drifted off. "It scares me sometimes."

"But you can change all that, Rhea." Zendar's hand went out across the table. He held her wrist. "I'm going to the cave. You could come with me."

Rhea withdrew her arm. "Not anymore. I haven't got the interest or the strength to make the climb, Zendar."

Zendar was disappointed. "Then give me directions, because I have to go."

There was something in the tone of his voice. His eyes seemed so familiar to her, and he was so sincere that she wanted to help him. "I'll take you to Akros," she said. "It would give me a feeling of participating in some small way." Rhea brightened.

"Then tomorrow's the day, Rhea."

"I don't know if I can take the day off. I have so much to do." She thought about it for a minute and then added, "Well, OK, I'll make time for it." She was more cheerful now. The thought of a change of pace lifted her. "I'll let my secretary know that I won't be in in the morning." She smiled. "Actually, I love the drive to the country. We'll make it an adventure! I'm not a climber, but I think I know the essentials. I'd love to help outfit you."

When the waitress returned, they ordered dinner and lapsed into silence. Rhea had thought it might become uncomfortable after that, but it wasn't. Even their silence was pleasant. Zendar was easy to be around. They ate quietly together, each anticipating their own idea of what was to come. Their energy blended well together.

"Old friends," Élan thought as he watched the two of them engaged in their own thoughts. He loved them both so much. He felt as if he could almost reach out and touch them in the transmission. For a moment it was like old times with just the three of them.

He watched as Zendar paid the bill and walked Rhea out to her car behind the restaurant. Zendar told her where he was staying, and they agreed to meet there at eight the next morning. They would have breakfast together, and by then the surplus store would be open. Zendar helped her into her car and leaned on the door as they said good-night. Rhea turned to watch him as he walked away from the car. "Who are you Zendar?" she wondered, "and why do I feel so comfortable with you, a perfect stranger?"

Walking back through the restaurant, Zendar exited onto the front street so that he could follow his now tattered map. The night air was cool and pleasantly refreshing. The sounds of city traffic had disappeared, and Zendar became momentarily immersed in the sensations of movement and walking. There was something fascinating about the way his arms and legs propelled him forward. The blocks passed quickly, and he soon found himself standing in front of an old stone building with an overhanging white canopy. "This must be the hotel," he said, entering the lobby.

The man at the desk registered Zendar, took his credit card, and pointed the way to the elevator.

As the elevator doors closed behind him, he pressed the seventh-floor button, and leaned back against the wall. The stately steel and wood enclosure creaked and started upwards.

Still overwhelmed by the mixture of emotions and weary from his encounter with Rhea, Zendar headed for his room. That night he fell into a deep sleep. In his dream, the mountain loomed before him, and his heart beat fast as he approached the path. As he waved good-bye to Rhea in his dream, he noticed that there were tears streaming down her cheeks. Then a song whispered in the wind on the mountainside. It called to Zendar's soul, and he turned to face the narrow path alone.

Chapter 15

The Promise

Zendar was up at the crack of dawn and downstairs waiting for Rhea. She pulled up in a small white sports car just as he finished checking out. The top was down, and he couldn't help but notice how lovely she looked as he slid onto the gray leather seat beside her. She was wearing blue denim jeans and a soft yellow blouse that accented her dark eyes and billowed in the wind as she shifted into high gear and headed onto the freeway.

Breakfast was pleasant. She helped him pick from the menu at a small truck stop: scrambled eggs, hash browns, toast and coffee. They didn't talk much, but they didn't need to. Being together was enough.

The surplus store was in an older part of town. Rhea made the process fun and easy. Becoming the perfect escort as they entered the door, she grabbed a shopping cart and started down the aisles, chattering all the while about the coming event. He followed behind her, dipping into the conversation now and then just to keep it going. She was the promoter and guide, taking full responsibility for the event. He enjoyed watching her, totally alive and animated now. This had been the energy he'd sensed in her eyes, a youthful vitality she'd thought she'd lost.

By the time they were finished, his basket was full. She kept it basic: a knapsack, army knife, rope, grappling hook, gloves, climbing boots, flashlight and batteries, a heavy jacket for the night, and two canteens that he filled from the faucet behind the back of the store. They stopped to pick up some staples at a grocery store on the way out of town and put the convertible top up before leaving the parking lot.

By ten-thirty they turned onto the interstate and headed east out of town. During the ride, she became especially animated, her conversation filled with hope for his quest. Zendar wondered if she was talking about it to relieve her own anxiety about the choice she'd made.

"Why don't you just come with me Rhea?" he blurted out abruptly, interrupting one of her run-on sentences. "You know you want to."

"I'm sorry, Zendar." The tension released from her shoulders. "I was chattering on and on, wasn't I?" She glanced over at him as she turned the wheel and pulled around a large truck that was slowing their progress. "It's silly. I hadn't thought about the quest in years. Just being with you has restored some of my old vigor. I guess it's like a vicarious experience. Your going to the mountain is giving me a feeling of going too. Maybe I'm just trying to push back my own feelings of guilt."

"Guilt over what?" Zendar didn't understand.

"Guilt over not going."

"Then come."

"You know I can't."

Zendar decided not to press her. He was sorry that she didn't see the opportunity. He had been delivered to her. But she was incapable of seeing the perfection in it right now.

In the course room, Élan began to pace. "Oh, Zendar," he thought, "if only she'd recognize the gift." It was the sirens' song that Rhea was singing; the pull of the world was too strong in her now.

Zendar had wanted so badly for her to come on the journey. He sighed and turned away, directing his attention out the window. "She was right last night when she said she was caught." He turned to look at her from the side. He was so sorry. She was such a lovely lady, but she was lost to the power of the city.

Rhea was lost in her own world, unaware of Zendar's withdrawal. "I do want to find the cave," she said, turning momentarily to look at him. "Maybe I will someday, later in my life . . ." her voice trailed off as she spoke.

"I hear you, Rhea," he said gently, and this time he really did. "I understand what you're trying to say."

"You do?" she said, relieved.

"Maybe it's a time of preparation for you, a time

to strengthen yourself, so that when your time does come to make the ascent, you'll be ready."

"That's it!" Rhea was relieved to be let off the hook. "Oh, thank you for understanding, I didn't want to feel guilty because I can't go."

"Of course not. There's no reason for guilt. I'm sure that you know exactly what you're doing." He shifted his voice, dropping it an octave lower as he continued, "But do be careful, Rhea, you can't stay too long and not be trapped for good."

"I know." She was ready to change the subject.

Zendar wondered if it wasn't already too late. Rhea was mesmerized, her arguments solid. He gazed out of his window as they drifted into silence. There were foothills everywhere now, rolling green hills dotted with occasional trees.

"Open the glove compartment, Zendar." Rhea interrupted his thoughts, pointing to the compartment at his knee. "I think I left a map in there from my last trip to the country."

He reached into a pile of papers and pulled out a map. "Is this it?"

"Looks like it. Open it and see if you can find the exit to Mount Akros," she said. "It feels like we've been driving awhile, and it should be coming up real soon."

"Here it is," Zendar said, pointing to a spot on the map. "Exit number seventy-two."

"Oh good, we just passed number seventy. It should be any minute now."

It was early afternoon when the highway made a sharp right angle and swung around the foothills. Before them and to their right was a long, flat plain, and beyond it a towering mountain. Five minutes later they pulled off the main highway onto Exit 72. They were deep in the country now, approximately four miles from the base of the mountain.

It loomed larger and larger before them as they sped over the country road. It was far more beautiful than Zendar had imagined. He leaned out of the car window to peer at the mountain. Its massive body was awe-inspiring, spreading at the base, rising to a sheer stone cliff at her heights, where her crest of glacial ice shimmered like crystal in the afternoon sun. Zendar gasped. He felt the lure of his lifetime goal stirring in the center of his chest. Like some great magnetic force, he could feel the mountain's pull. He was bound by her spell, captivated by her charm, lured by her power.

"She's calling me, Rhea," he whispered. He was leaning forward in his seat to look at Mount Akros through the front window. "I can feel her drawing me into her."

Exit 72 turned into a dirt road that led directly to the base of the mountain. As Rhea slowed the car she turned to look at Zendar's face. He was studying the mountain at close range now. His tawny brown hair was streaked in gold from the sunlight, and his aquiline features combined with his purity of intent touched her. For a moment, Rhea was envious.

Where the mountain called to him, it seemed to spurn her. Where its majestic towering cliffs invited him to her, she found those same cliffs a powerful force to be revered but avoided. In her heart, she almost wished that the mountain were calling her, for she knew that until it did, she would not be ready to make the climb.

"Oh, Rhea." His words cut into her silent reverie. "I am bound to the mountain now, as a child is bound to its mother before birthing. I feel as if she holds a covenant, a promise, a hope for something new."

The car moved slowly over gravel as they approached the base of the mountain. The road veered sharply to the right and came to a dead halt twenty feet beyond the turn. A wire fence with a guard gate blocked their way. Rhea parked the car about three feet from the steel bars where a no-trespassing sign was hanging on the fence in front of them.

Zendar looked over at her. "This is it!" His heart was pounding as he reached for the door handle and got out of the car.

Rhea watched as he walked around the front of the car and rested his hands on the gate. As he leaned on the fence, his head went up to take a long look at the mountain before him, and she noticed that his back was strong, perfectly built. "He's left already," she thought. His soul was bound to this path of purpose that seemed nearly within his reach now. Watching him at a distance, she admired his singleness of focus. His heart had been captivated by the goal that she now avoided. She opened her door and walked around the car to join him at the gate.

"We should pack your things into the knapsack," she said, leaning on the fence beside him.

"I forgot." Zendar was torn. He felt the pull of the mountain, but he also felt Rhea's pull.

They walked over to the car and got the bags out of the backseat. Rhea knelt on the ground and unwrapped the items they had purchased, removing the price tags one by one. Her dark hair fell forward around her face as she worked. Zendar couldn't take his eyes off her. There was a mysterious quality about her, a unique blend of strength and softness. He was sorry that the city lured her, sorry she was captivated by the world.

Back in the course room, Elder Em knew that Zendar and Rhea would part soon. He was disappointed. Rhea had called to him, and now she turned him down. Why couldn't she recognize the help she had asked for? Soon his chance would be over. He needed to make one last attempt to reach her. "Try it one more time Zendar," he murmured intently under his breath as he stared up at the transmission. "Try it again, my friend."

Zendar was suddenly overwhelmed with emotion. "Come with me," he blurted out as he threw himself on his knees beside her.

Rhea was startled at his outburst. She stared into

his blue eyes for a long moment before answering. "This is not my journey, Zendar," she said finally. "This is your journey and your goal."

"It's meant for both of us, Rhea. You always wanted to find the cave and now we're here at the base of the mountain. We could find it together. I know we could." Zendar was bending over his knapsack, leaning toward her on both knees now.

He looked so boyish that Rhea's heart was moved. "Oh Zendar." She was torn, but the pull of the city was greater. "I've worked too hard to get where I am. I haven't got the will to leave," she said finally. "And I just can't seem to create it."

Zendar looked into her brown eyes, stood, and reached down to take her hand. "I wish you'd change your mind and go with me," he said quietly as he helped her up.

Rhea dusted off her jeans as she stood beside him. "I'll climb the fence with you," she said. "And I'll walk with you to the end of the dirt road where the trail begins." She reached down and picked up the knapsack. "But where the trail begins is where I turn back and you continue on your journey alone." She handed him the pack as she spoke.

Rhea locked the car and together they walked back to the gate. With Zendar's help she swung herself over onto the other side. Zendar handed the knapsack over the fence to her, and he followed.

"We can make it together Rhea."

"I'm not so sure." She was looking up at him, her

voice distant and apart. "I think it's a path that every soul must walk alone." She looked toward the mountain. "Maybe my time will come someday, but it's not now."

As Zendar looked into Rhea's eyes, he couldn't help but be drawn to her. She was disarmingly lovely, even though she was lost to him now. His hands gently dropped from her shoulders. He had to let her go. He turned and they began to walk together once again.

The deep hush of the mountain fell like a blanket around them as they advanced along the dusty road in silence, each lost in private thoughts. Now and then birds would chirp in the bushes along the side of the road, but otherwise there was only the wide, deep silence of the country. The sun followed at an angle behind them casting long shadowy phantoms that scattered in the dust at their feet.

The dirt trail turned suddenly to the left and ended abruptly in a thicket of bushes. From that point only a thin footpath cut through the brambles. Rhea turned to Zendar, her eyes wide with realization. This was the turning point. From here one soul would go on and one would turn back, each bound by a different calling.

Zendar looked down at Rhea as her eyes suddenly filled with tears. "I really wish that I could go." She looked unexpectedly small and vulnerable standing there gazing up at him with regret in her eyes.

"So do I, Rhea." But he knew she had already chosen.

"Oh, Zendar," her voice quivered. "Sometimes I'm so afraid."

"Afraid of what?" Zendar reached for her.

"Afraid that I won't make it, afraid that I really am caught, and that I won't ever get free."

"But Rhea, you just said it wasn't your time." He held her to his chest now.

"I know" she said, "but now with you leaving, I'm not so sure of myself." She pressed her head against his shoulder.

"I understand." He gently stroked her head.

She stepped back and looked up into his eyes. "Will you come back for me, Zendar?"

Zendar was shocked. "Come back for you?"

"Please!"

"I can't do that Rhea."

"Yes you can," she insisted. "After you've found the cave, come back for me."

"Rhea, don't ask that of me, please."

"But I'm afraid Zendar. I won't be able to make it alone." She gazed up at the mountain. "I'm not strong enough. I need you."

A bolt of pain went through Zendar's chest. "Don't ask this of me, Rhea, please. I can't say what will happen to me once I find the cave."

"Promise me," she begged. "Please promise me that you'll come back and help me."

"But why?"

"I need your strength to reach the goal."

"What do you mean?"

"Well, if you find the cave maybe you can help me find it too."

"I can't do that, Rhea. I don't know what's going to happen on the mountain."

"Please," she pleaded. "If you'll just promise, I'll rest secure knowing that one day I'll attain the goal, too." She grabbed his hand now. "Please, Zendar, please promise you'll come back for me."

Overwhelmed by the rush of her emotions and flooded with tenderness, Zendar looked at her, his heart torn.

"But Rhea . . ."

"I'm begging you, Zendar."

Her sudden vulnerability disarmed him. "I promise, Rhea," he said with quiet acceptance. "I promise to return and find you."

"Oh, thank you." Rhea smiled in relief as she released his hand. Excited now, she was already anticipating his return. "Just knowing that you'll come back relieves my fears! Knowing I have someone I can depend on helps me."

He reached down to stroke her hair lightly. "You're a beautiful woman, Rhea."

"Now I'm encouraged Zendar." Her face lit up. "I know you're going to do it. Just go up there and fulfill your quest, and remember that I'll be back here waiting for you."

"Good-bye, Rhea," he said.

"Bless you, Zendar." She smiled mysteriously. "And Zendar," she said quietly, "walk with angels."

"Walk with angels?" he wondered.

"My mother used to tell me that. Whenever I was in need of help. When I had a test to pass at school or a challenge to face, she'd always kiss me at the door and say, 'Walk with angels, Rhea, and be strong.'"

"Thank you," he said, shifting his knapsack on his shoulders. "Walk with angels, Rhea, and be strong," he whispered quietly, turning to face the trail alone.

"You too, my friend! My heart goes with you."

A slight breeze caught her hair as he turned to wave his last good-bye. The brambles of the thicket soon swallowed him from sight, and he disappeared into the bush. Rhea listened until the final rustling faded into the din of country sounds, and then she turned back on the road in the direction of her parked car.

She wondered how Zendar would look the next time they met. Would he be different in any way? Would he be more radiant? Would he be lit with the flame of awakening? Would she recognize him by his walk, his laugh, or the light in his eyes? Or would everything have changed?

As Rhea reached her car, she stopped for a moment and turned back in silence. Holding her love for Zendar in her heart, she offered it up to the mountain, praying that it would deliver its ancient secret to her friend and release him into her heart.

Chapter 16

A Night on the Mountain

Zendar's walk was purposeful as he cut through the trail. In the beginning his heart was heavy with separation, but as he progressed the path with its dense overgrowth took all of his attention. Soon his mind was on the mission before him.

After about twenty minutes, the bushes finally opened into a clearing. Ahead of him was the base of the mountain. From a distance he had seen that there were patches of trees sprinkling the bottom third of the mountain, but from where he stood now, the trees looked like an immense forest. As he entered it, the sun was starkly shadowed, falling around him in mottled patches as he walked.

Zendar became lost in the world of the senses as the forest enveloped him in a dancing kaleidoscope of hues and multicolored tones. Splotches of light and dark, cold and warm sent tremors through his body as he moved.

He was amazed at the range of color and feelings that rippled through his skin, sending signals to his mind. He was awestruck at the sensitivity of the body to subtle shifts in sensation, and he became mesmerized by the change that took place in visual perception as he walked from shadows into light.

For awhile he was immersed in testing the differences. Closing his eyes for moments at a time as he walked, he focused on the changes in light and dark, warm and cool as they played through his eyelids. Soon he found that closing his eyes heightened his sense of hearing and the sensations that played across his skin.

He felt the soil give beneath his feet as he tested walking with his eyes half-closed, and focused inward. As he played with perception, he got better and better at detecting fine distinctions in sensations. Soon he touched the intuitive realm where feelings blend with inner knowing. He discovered that he could sense tree stumps that blocked the path before him. And if he held his awareness very still, he could feel branches that hung across his path ahead of him.

In this manner he moved through the forest region quickly, finally arriving at an area where the trees grew sparse. Shale and stone met his feet as the climb grew suddenly steeper. Zendar sat on a gray slab of rock to change into his boots. Leaving his walking shoes on a large boulder as a marker for his return, he stood to test his new leather climbing boots. The mountain was carved in stark granite rising at a forty-five-degree angle before him. Zendar viewed the terrain, looking for a passage through the massive rock.

Finding a trail to his right, he began the steep ascent, lacing his way along the path of least resistance as he climbed. Soon every part of his body was engaged in the jagged endeavor. He used his hands and arms to pull himself up onto ledges and his feet to test for loose stones as he made his way along the rocky face of the lower mountain.

The tree line was at a distance below him when he finally stopped to rest on a boulder. Wiping his brow, he opened one of the canteens and took a long, slow drink. He was high enough to see the city at a distance now. The sun hung at a four o'clock angle in the sky, casting late afternoon tones across the buildings. Zendar thought of Rhea. Where was she? She must be home by now. "Rhea," he whispered beneath his breath, "life is a sacred journey. Don't lose sight of the goal." He prayed for her safekeeping. "It is the purpose and the goal that binds us together," he thought. "I must find the Cave of Compassion." If he could find it, then she could get there too.

Raising his knapsack back onto his shoulders, Zendar stood to face the trail again. The thin rocky path that had led steadily upward from the forest now dwindled into a barely discernible trail, ending at the base of a towering granite cliff. The only way was straight up. Before him, vertical rock-cliff walls shot straight into the air like the walls of a citadel shielding any traveler from entry into the heart of the mountain. Realizing that the tests were awaiting him somewhere up on the high peaks, he scanned the vast stone embankment, trying to calculate a place to make his ascent.

Spotting a ledge about thirty feet in the air, he used the rope and hook to inch his way upward, finally arriving about twelve feet from the first overhanging mantle. His first attempts at controlling the aim of his throw were clumsy, but eventually he was able to anchor the grappling hook firmly enough into the rock to hold his weight. Climbing hand over hand, he pulled himself onto the ledge.

He lay on the first shelf for some time, feeling the warm shale and stone beneath his cheek, but finally the desire for the goal overtook the tiredness in his body. Taking a moment to replenish with water, he stood to view the next outcropping some ten feet above his head.

Zendar painstakingly inched his way slowly up the cliff walls, moving from ledge to ledge, slicing out a fine but thinning trail of hope as he climbed. During the earlier stages of the climb, his heart had been high with anticipation. Now, as his pace slowed to a crawl, thoughts ricocheted against the walls of his mind and the fire of hope began to wane. Either the rock walls were solidly shielding a secret, or the tale of the mountain was a legend, he thought, for nowhere could he see an opening or an indentation in the hard wall.

As the early rays of sunset tinted the western sky, Zendar rolled his rope in his right hand once again and prepared for the throw. Although his arms were feeling the strain of the afternoon, his aim was sure now, and he began his climb, hand over hand to the next ledge. Suddenly, about four inches below the landing, Zendar felt the hook slip and the rope give. Reaching up he grabbed hold of jutting rock, and pulling with every ounce of strength left in his arms, he hoisted himself onto the shelf. He rolled over into the ledge, and as he did, the hook and rope dislodged completely and careened down the cliff.

Zendar felt a sudden surge of energy in his chest as a scream split the air. He spun around to see who was there, but the shelf was empty.

Back in the course room Élan was holding onto the edge of his desk, riveted to the transmission. No one in the class moved. Their friend was trapped a thousand feet in the air with no way up and no way down.

Studying his predicament now, Zendar noticed that the shelf was about four feet deep. Pulling himself back, he propped himself against the mountain wall to consider his alternatives.

"He doesn't have any alternatives!" interjected Justin impetuously. "Maybe we should call Rhea. She could rescue him."

On the ledge, leaning against the mountain wall, Zendar thought of Rhea, and wondered if she would ever think to find him or would he die alone up here.

"Trust, Zendar," Élan whispered. "You taught me to trust," he said. "Please use the teaching now."

Zendar watched darkness devour the mountain in stages. It began behind the city in violet and indigo, consuming the borders of the western sky. Then it crept toward him across the roof of day, finally swallowing the afternoon light from one horizon line to another. With only luminous stars spattering the cobalt sky, Zendar now stared into a gaping pitch black hole, facing a night in the belly of darkness.

Zendar lay on the ledge shrouded in solitude. His mind reeled back in time through his journey. The city streets teeming with people. Horns and sirens screaming. The lady in the information booth at Daltons. Rhea's eyes as she shared her story over dinner. Rhea's eyes filled with tears at parting. Then outer reality snapped as visions flashed and fused before him. Rhea in the stars overhead.

"Rhea," Zendar cried out loud as he fell forward on his knees to grab her. But her face dissolved into mist, and he found himself on the ledge alone. He lay on the barren rock wringing with perspiration. Suddenly his awareness plummeted, breaking the surface soil of consciousness, he plunged downward through a dark tunnel into an inner cavern of destinies and dreams. At the far end of the underground cavity he could see a pool. Lit by a strange inner light, the strain of a melody emerged from its waters. It was his soul's song that was drawing him in.

Fleeting memories floated by: *a filmy feeling of a stellar home; milky clouds outside a classroom window; a misty image of a face surrounded by flowing silver hair. Voices chanting from a distant source, blending with his heart like a drumbeat on the border of his mind.*

"Remember, remember, remember . . ." The boundaries of his body exploded into stars that splattered across the ceiling of his inner vision, and a great battlefield rolled open before him.

Zendar plunged into despair as he viewed the landscape of a thousand foes. The flame of hope confronted the searing fire of fear. The ego and the soul were now locked in deadly conflict for control of the mind of a man.

Like ancient dinosaurs rising from a mighty sleep, resignation and lethargy attacked from the right, while apathy and indifference charged from the left. Should he have turned back? Was the quest a dream? Why am I here alone?

The forces of darkness raged against the forces of light, and old choices not yet complete returned in phantom form to tempt him. Should he have stayed with Rhea? Was the timing wrong? Did he make a mistake? Was it really his ego that led him here? Was the cave really a rumor? Was the path a fatal dream?

In a final fight for freedom, he reached deep for the source within. Amidst the wailing images of war, he felt the burning flame of hope rising in his heart. He saw his commitment to the goal driving him on. His mind staggered and tottered in confusion.

"If trying and giving it your all doesn't work, what does?" he whispered.

"I gave everything," he screamed out loud, "and it wasn't enough!"

Stars danced against an icy sapphire sky, as Zendar's voice fell into the cold black void just beyond the ledge.

"What do you want from me?" he screamed up at the ceiling above his head.

"I'm a man, but I'm only a man. There's no more that I can do!"

As the silence swallowed his words, Zendar pleaded to the heavens.

"Help me," he called. "I'm trapped with no way up and no way down."

The course room was plunged into despair as Zendar's heart filled the atmosphere; his trials were their trials, his agony their agony. Zendar's body was weak. "Help me," he said finally. "I surrender!"

As the words left his mouth, the cliff rock that had been cradling his spine, shook and shifted. Zendar rolled backwards into a gaping opening in the wall.

"It's the cave," whispered Élan. "Oh Zendar, you've found the cave."

Chapter 17

The Cave

Zendar lay on his back looking up in shock at a huge cavernous rock ceiling above his head. "It's the cave," he whispered.

He turned onto his side and sat up. The grotto was cool and resonated with a gentle sound he'd heard before. The entire scene was lit by a luminous glow. The cave's ceiling towered about fifty feet above his head like a vaulted cathedral, an ancient womb bearing a hidden mystery.

As his eyes adjusted to the light, Zendar could make out a familiar figure in a long gray robe. He stood facing Zendar at the far end of the cave. Behind the figure and to his left were four large round stones approximately eighteen inches in diameter. To his right were four other stones of matching size. Directly behind him stood a great stone. It towered a full three feet higher than the figure. In front were two high back wooden chairs placed side by side facing the great stone

As Zendar's eyes adjusted to the light, he could make out the hair and face of Raoul.

"Come Zendar," he said. His voice reverberated off the walls of the rock chamber. "I've been waiting for you."

"Raoul." Zendar started toward him, mesmerized by the energy in the vaulted room. "What are you doing here?"

"I live here," he answered.

"In the cave?"

"No." He gestured to the two chairs. "Come," he said, "sit with me and I'll explain."

Zendar walked around to the front of the seats. "It's good to see you," he said as he seated himself.

Raoul sat beside him in the other chair. "You too," he said, touching the young man's shoulder.

The stones now faced them in a semicircle and Zendar could see that each bore an inscription. As he read each stone, fleeting images began to return.

"The window between the worlds stands open to you now," Raoul said. "You have accomplished your goal. Your amnesia is dissolving."

Zendar sat staring at the stones in amazement. As he read each one, he began to see through the veil of time. To his left the first stone bore the word REMEMBER. As he read it he saw Élan perched in his window seat gazing into the vapors beyond and the jewel of spirit in his dream. As Zendar read the second stone, LISTEN he saw Jaron in the boat with James. Little by little his memory returned with each stone. ASK—He saw Élan in the river and Jaron fighting the storm at sea. BE STILL, SEE, ACT—Justin and Ashley suddenly were surrounded by the gang. Then there were the final stones of BELIEVE and SURREN-

DER. Zendar's mind reeled as he heard Rhea's voice: "Promise you'll come back for me." Her dark brown eyes suddenly penetrated his heart.

"I didn't realize it," Zendar gasped, falling back into his seat. "It's her. It's *our* Rhea." His eyes searched Raoul's face. "That's why she seemed so familiar to me."

"None of us are strangers," Raoul smiled. "Do you understand?"

"I think so," Zendar answered. "But this is really a lot to grasp in one quick awakening. Help me, Raoul."

"Do you remember the training and the simulations now, Zendar?" Raoul asked.

"I'm beginning to." Zendar could see the training room in his mind's eye as he spoke. "It's all coming back to me now, sir."

"The training and the simulations are a metaphor for life," Raoul began slowly. He was watching Zendar closely, gauging his reactions as he spoke. "Planet Earth really is a classroom. Every thing that happens there is for a lesson. Just as everything we did on the other side was part of the training, so everything on Earth is part of Earth's training." Raoul paused.

"In our real lives, the ones that we live on Earth, simulations come to us in the form of life events. Each time you remember to remember who you are in a life event, and you act accordingly, you pass one of life's simulations."

Zendar leaned forward, his eyes searching the earth floor as he felt the power of Raoul's teaching.

"All of life is a dream, Zendar." Raoul's voice was resonant. "And we only awaken from the amnesia when we completely surrender."

"Surrender?" Zendar stared into Raoul's eyes. "You mean like I did on the ledge?"

"Like you did on the ledge." Raoul nodded in assent.

"And then what?" Zendar turned toward his teacher. "After surrender, what?"

"Look," Raoul said, gesturing to the great stone. Zendar sat back and looked up as the word PURPOSE appeared etched in large silver letters on the stone.

"This is the last great secret," Raoul said. "At least this is the last great secret that you'll receive before birth." Raoul looked up to a spot above the great stone as he continued. "Are you watching closely, Élan?"

Zendar looked over at Raoul, puzzled. "I'm Zendar, sir."

"I know, but I was also talking with Élan and the rest of the group." Raoul pointed high above the boulder, and there in the transmission was the entire class watching Zendar look up at them.

"Wow, I really missed all of you," Zendar exclaimed.

"We never let go of you, Zendar," Élan answered. "We were with you the whole time."

"But I couldn't see you, so I didn't know it," Zendar replied.

"Just as Earth people don't know that their loved ones who live beyond the window of time are always with them," Élan said.

Zendar breathed. He remembered Élan's simulation and how they had all supported him in spirit. "You were helping me, weren't you?"

"You make it easy, Zendar," Élan smiled. "You're quite open and receptive."

"Are you ready to go on now?" Raoul interceded gently. Élan and Zendar both nodded.

"Purpose," Raoul said. "I want to discuss the meaning of this word." He stood and walked over to the great stone. "Every child who is born on Earth comes with three things." Raoul tapped the face of the rock and three lines appeared beneath the word *purpose*.

GIFTS AND TALENTS
CONTRIBUTION
LESSONS

Pointing to the words as he spoke, Raoul continued. "The first of these is gifts and talents," he said. "Every child is born with special gifts and talents, and every child unconsciously knows what these gifts and talents are. Secondly, all souls enter Earth with a specific contribution to make," he said. "In other words, each child has a special contribution to give with the gifts and talents that they've been given. And finally, all souls come to learn lessons." Raoul's right hand gestured in the direction of the final word on the rock face.

"As we said before," he continued, "these lessons come in the form of life events. Therefore, every person on Earth has a special place where they fit in the scheme of things. They come bearing gifts and talents that, when developed, will help them make a contribution to the whole. During their lifetime of contribution, lessons will arise naturally out of the nature of the challenge of the human ego and free will." Raoul paused, addressing Zendar. "You do remember the ego and free will, don't you?"

"How could I ever forget?" Zendar answered.

"Well," Raoul responded, "many human beings do forget, Zendar. That's the reason we initiated the plan."

"Is that clear for those of you up there?" Raoul now addressed the rest of the students. "Justin?"

"I think I'm clear, Raoul." Justin hadn't expected to be called on.

"Brooke?"

"No questions at the moment, sir," Brooke answered.

"How about the rest of you? Ashley?" Raoul looked over at her. She was seated next to Justin toward the back of the room.

"I do have a question, Raoul," she said. "Could you

explain the gifts. What exactly are they and how do we recognize them?"

"Great question." Raoul walked over to his chair and seated himself. "Let's talk about the simulation for a moment. How many of you noticed that you had some special gifts during the simulation?" Jaron and Élan looked puzzled.

"I don't understand," Justin called out.

"I think I do." Zendar sat forward in his seat. "Can I try?"

"Please," Raoul nodded.

"I can't really tell you about my gifts, Raoul, but I can tell you what I feel about the ones I love."

"Perfect, Zendar," he said. "Tell me what you see in Élan."

Élan leaned forward with interest as Zendar began to speak. "Well, sir, Élan has a special spirit, a special zest and enthusiasm that he brings to every thing he does."

Élan smiled, touched at Zendar's response. He'd never heard him speak this way.

"Élan is always willing, and he applies himself completely to every task that he takes on." Zendar paused thoughtfully. "Élan is ever ready to face the unknown with enthusiasm and intention. His gifts center around the joy that he brings to the quest." Zendar looked up at the transmission. "There's a lot more I could say about my friend, but is that what you're getting at, Raoul?"

"Exactly." Raoul nodded and turned to Ashley.

"Do you understand? We can often recognize our gifts through the eyes of our friends and loved ones?"

"Thank you, Raoul," Ashley answered quietly.

"OK, my turn." Élan said, standing up and looking at Raoul in the transmission. "May I do Zendar?"

"Of course." Raoul was pleased.

"Zendar," Élan's voice was reflective as he felt his friend's energy, "is courageous. He has strength of intention and strong commitment. He is very disciplined. Zendar will never leave a task incomplete, and he's sometimes careful in taking on new challenges because he knows that he must finish what he starts." He smiled inwardly. "Zendar's power of concentration surpasses any other that I've seen. He is insightful, clear-headed, and focused. I have found him to be a most dear and loyal friend." Élan stopped and addressed Zendar directly now. "Thank you for all that you give, my friend."

Justin called out, "I want to share about Ashley's gifts. Ashley is sensitive and refined. Sometimes people don't recognize her inner strength, because of her outer demeanor. She has a tremendous depth about her. She has an insatiable thirst to understand. She always penetrates to the depths of a situation or a person, and this quality gives wisdom to her actions." Justin sat back, and then leaned forward again as if he'd just remembered something else. "One more thing." He gestured with his right hand. "Ashley has the remarkable ability to pull through under tremendous duress." Justin relaxed into his chair, satisfied that he'd gotten it.

"Excellent!" Raoul was impressed with their candor, but it was the mutual respect and support that struck him the most. This would be the very thing that would bring the team together and keep them together later. Looking up at the transmission he continued, "Each of you needs to understand your importance to the plan and to each other. Zendar is centered and strong, Justin is feisty, Ashley is insightful, Jaron is open-minded and resourceful, and Élan brings his enthusiasm to every adventure. Each of you will take the lead at different times, but each of you is important to the mission and the goal."

"What about the rest of us?" Brooke interjected.

"Each and every one of you is important to the plan." Raoul smiled. He hadn't meant to be exclusive. "Not a soul is left out," he said with certainty. Noticing that Brooke was still unsettled, he added, "One of your special gifts is stability, Brooke. It will be something that the team needs, and you will be there for them."

"I've always seen that quality in you," Jaron added. "I depend on it." Brooke smiled and sat back in her seat. She did know that about herself.

"The plan will unfold in due time," Raoul confirmed. Brooke nodded. She had an inner certainty about her role, even though it wasn't yet evident. Raoul turned and gestured to the entire group. "Are there any further questions?"

"Not from me," Justin answered.

"I have another question," Ashley ventured. Justin smiled. That was the unquenchable thirst for knowledge he so admired in her. "What's the difference between gifts and talents?"

"That's a good one! They're very similar," Raoul said. "The difference is that gifts are aspects of character such as the ones mentioned, while talents can be honed into a skill or an art form. In other words, we use our gifts to hone our talents, and in the process of doing so we further develop our gifts of character."

"So the mechanical ability or the ability to sing or write or dance, all of these are talents?" Ashley interjected.

"Right."

"And we develop our gifts of character such as courage or discipline in the process of perfecting our talents?" Ashley asked.

"Correct," Raoul answered. "In this way our gifts and talents support each other. We can develop patience, discipline, and commitment to a goal while we're honing our talents of dance, counseling, or drawing, for example."

"And we come to Earth to develop both?" Ashley asked.

"Yes," Raoul answered. "For the purpose of contribution to the greater whole."

"Thank you, Raoul." Ashley sat back, complete.

Raoul nodded. "Are there any other questions?"

When there was no response, he turned to Zendar. "So, my friend, this is it.

"After all your course of study, what conclusions have you drawn about the nature of being human?" Raoul smiled as he looked the young man in the eye. "I guess what I'm really asking, Zendar, is, 'What does it really mean to be a human being?' "

"What does it *really* mean to be a human being . . . ," Zendar said slowly. "I have found, in my experience, that questions are more powerful than answers. And this particular question is the most important question ever asked by any human being down through time."

"Explain."

Zendar stared at the earth floor and asked for help as he gathered his thoughts. "I believe, sir, that the question, 'what does it mean to be a human being' is an eternal question, yet at one and the same time it is a profoundly personal one. It is a question that lies at the center of man's search for meaning, his search to understand himself in relationship to his world . . . his family, his community, his country, and the universe at large." Zendar paused and looked up. He could feel Élan's eyes on him. His support was reassuring.

He turned back to face the teacher, noting how impressive he looked in his gray robe that flowed in folds over the arms of his chair. "This question is at the heart of the course curriculum for all human beings on Planet Earth." Zendar paused. "Down through the ages, great teachers and thinkers have wrestled with it, and it is in this wrestling to understand that each of their personal truths has been revealed."

"How is that?"

"You taught us of Gandhi, sir. When Gandhi sought to answer this question for himself, it clarified his purpose. For Gandhi, to be a human being was to be free."

"So freedom is the answer."

"It's not that simple."

"Go on."

"Freedom is an aspect of the answer, but to give a pat answer to that question could lead to dogma, sir. The power of the question lies in the fact that it has no singular answer. The question is a living question. It belongs to every one and must be answered in the living of our lives." Zendar stilled his mind and focused his attention beyond the window of time so that Earth's history began to unfold before his inner eye. "By asking what it really means to be a human being, Gandhi lived a simple life in a profound way. But there were other great individuals who answered the question through their lives," he said. "By Michaelangelo's hand and eye, David became the perfect man. In René Descartes' estimation, man's greatest gift was his ability to think. 'I think therefore I am,' he said. Marcus Aurelius believed that the arrow of one's life should be ever focused on the attainment of virtue, while Plato felt that the goals of life were truth, beauty, and goodness. Leonardo da Vinci answered the question in his perfectly proportioned human being, who served as a symbol of spiritual, mental, emotional, and physical balance. And there were thousands of others, both known and unknown. Wherever we see a simple life lived in an extraordinary way, the question has been there serving as a context for the content of a person's actions."

"Outstanding, Zendar." Raoul couldn't hide his pleasure. Zendar's lucid interpretation of complex concepts was impressive. "But what about purpose? How does it fit in all of this?"

"The question, 'What does it mean' establishes a context for our lives while purpose determines the content." Zendar could feel the power of his own insight. "As far as I can see, there are really two purposes on Earth." Zendar crossed his right foot over his left and leaned back against the boulder as he continued. "I like to think of these two as a planetary purpose and a personal purpose, Raoul. See if my interpretation is accurate." Zendar pushed away from the rock and looked up at the word *purpose*. "At times I'm going to use the word *mission* as synonymous with purpose in order to discuss the subject. Is that OK?" He looked over at Raoul.

"Go ahead." Raoul gestured an assent.

"OK. The planetary purpose or mission of every human being on earth is to live the law of unconditional love in action. This is the major mission of all individuals. Love breeds life in full abundance, and everyone on Earth has this mission or purpose in common."

Zendar looked up at Élan momentarily, feeling his thoughts. Élan was staring at him enraptured. He knew their time together was short now, and he wondered momentarily where each of their birth paths would lead. As Élan stared at his friend in the transmission, he vowed to find Zendar regardless of the distance between them at birth. Zendar winked, and it broke the intensity. Élan knew that it was Zendar's vow too.

Zendar turned back to face Raoul. "Then there are the minor missions. Every individual born on Earth has a personal purpose or minor mission to fulfill. This purpose is the contribution that person vows to make to the whole of the human family before birth."

"Give me some examples of what a minor mission might be." Raoul stroked his neck as he spoke.

"Well the minor missions might be such things as raising a good family, or becoming a singer while raising a family, or being a doctor, or practicing environmental engineering. All of those are the minor personal missions that each individual chooses to contribute to the good of the whole." Zendar paused. "It's also worthy to note that an individual may have two or three minor missions during his or her life."

"And how does a person's minor mission relate to

his or her major mission of unconditional love?" Raoul queried.

"It's not simply what we do but also how we do it that matters," Zendar answered reflectively. "And the 'how' refers to our major mission, the mission of love."

"Go on."

"It's not just about raising a family, or becoming a doctor. It's how we go about doing these things that counts. Our major mission is love. Love must be the target that guides the arrow of our actions. We must give our full love to whatever we do." Zendar paused. "Some people are constantly wishing they were doing something else."

"Such as . . ." Raoul pressed.

"OK." Zendar shook his head and considered. "For example, child rearing. Some mothers and fathers are torn by the desire for a career. Never fully at peace with their position, they play their roles half-heartedly. The unseen consequence of this energy is unconsciously felt by the family and picked up by the children."

"And?"

"And the children internalize the struggle, never finding peace themselves."

"What's the antidote?"

"Surrender," Zendar said, stepping away from the great stone. "We must learn to trust life and give ourselves to whatever task is set before us. Our planetary purpose is a moving target. We have to love whatever comes our way, do it with all our hearts, and do it well. Then life will deliver the next step in the progression of our unfolding." Zendar thought for a moment. " 'Am I doing what I'm doing with love?' That is always the deciding question that links one's minor mission to one's major mission."

"Your insights are clear and accurate, Zendar." Raoul looked up and signaled to Elder Em, who was standing against the back wall of the course room watching the exchange. He nodded his approval.

"Is that it then?" Zendar asked.

"That's it!" Raoul relaxed into his chair, satisfied.

"So can I ask a question now?" Zendar walked over and seated himself in the chair beside his teacher again.

Raoul smiled. Elder Em was right. This student was unusual. He had a wisdom beyond his years. "He'll make an exceptional teacher one day," he thought.

"Of course you can," he answered.

"Well then, Raoul, what about the original question?"

"What question was that?"

"The one we started when I entered the cave," Zendar answered. "The question about where you live." Raoul was looking at him inquisitively. "If this cave is not your home, Raoul, then where is it?"

"Life is a miraculous event, Zendar." Raoul looked pensively into his student's eyes.

"I understand that, sir," Zendar answered quietly.

Was Raoul hedging? "But you still haven't answered my question. If the cave isn't your home, where then?"

"Where is my home?" Raoul sighed, resting his elbows on the arms of the chair. "Where do I live?" He gazed reflectively into Zendar's eyes as he continued. "I live in the heart of every man and every woman, Zendar," he said. "I am the light of spirit. I am peace and wisdom, and I wait within until surrender calls me."

"You see, the cave is a metaphor, Zendar." Raoul's eyes were deep pools that danced with inner light. "The cave represents the heart of every human being," he said. "And I wait for each one to come home to me there."

"So when I achieve the goal on Earth and I'm fully awakened, I'll find you there?" Zendar asked.

"Not exactly."

"What then?"

"You'll find yourself there."

"Now *I* don't understand."

"That's because you haven't gotten there yet."

"How do you mean that?"

"We are the same." Raoul held Zendar's gaze. "When you arrive you'll discover that we are all one, not only in theory but in reality. The spirit that lives in you lives in me. On the outside we look different, but on the inside we are, and always have been, the same."

Silence echoed throughout the cave. No one

moved in the course room above the Great Stone. Even Zendar was quiet. This was more than even he had expected.

"It is done." Raoul's resonant voice broke the silence with gentle certainty. "The training is complete."

"I'm humbled, sir." The moment seemed to extend into eternity as the two sat in silence.

"Are you ready?" Raoul asked finally.

"I think so, sir."

Raoul extended his hand to his student. "Then take my hand, Zendar, and we'll go home." Zendar placed his left hand in the hand of the master and slowly the scene dissolved around them.

Chapter 18

The Soul's Great Adventure

The next thing Zendar knew, he and Raoul were standing side by side in the front of the course room. Élan wanted to rush to his friend's side, but it didn't feel right. Unlike the other returns, a hushed reverence filled the room this time. The amnesia had completely disappeared, and the awareness in the room alluded to an approaching juncture. Time and the students stood poised at the edge of a chasm between two worlds.

The swish of Elder Em's robe brushing the legs of the seats was the only sound that disturbed the silence. He moved through the rows slowly, deliberately calibrating the tension in the atmosphere. It was a moment of portent where preparation was about to meet destiny.

"Zendar," he said as he reached the front of the room. His right hand went out and Zendar met it as they embraced. Raoul stood back, radiant. Their love for one another was special.

"I think we did it, Elder Em." Zendar took a deep breath and stood back to look into his teacher's face.

"Indeed we did." Elder Em exchanged a knowing look with Raoul as he stepped forward to join them. It had gone better than either had planned. Zendar had excelled in his thesis. As a result, all of the students had received an astute analysis of the teaching from a peer.

"Life is a paradox," Zendar proceeded in his observations. "Where I thought I was traveling outwards in search of the cave, Elder Em, I was really on an inner journey through the landscape of my own being. And where I thought that I would be alone, in the cave, I found myself feeling full, at one with peace and wisdom." Zendar smiled at Raoul.

"You did well, my son," Elder Em concluded.

Zendar nodded. "And thank you, Raoul," he said, reaching for the master's hand before heading back to his seat. "I'll always remember you."

Elder Em knew that it was time for Raoul to leave. "Well, my friend, is there anything else that you want to say before you depart?"

"I think it has almost all been said." Raoul turned to face the class. "Your missions are just beginning," he said. "Only the training portion of the plan is complete. Remember that you will not be alone. Although you are the first class of trainees, you'll not be the last. Another wave of students will follow right behind you." Raoul smiled, raising his hand in farewell. "As you go through life, always remember that our goal is the transformation of consciousness on Earth. Your purpose is to bring about a renaissance of hope and wonder, a renaissance of good will among all human beings." With that,

Raoul dissolved and Elder Em was left standing at the front of the room alone.

"This is it!" the elder said. "All of our training has led us to this moment."

"Are we really about to be born?" Justin was dubious. Even though he'd expected this moment, he hadn't anticipated the reality of its arrival. Soon he would be bound on a journey of destiny. Where would that be?

"Yes," answered the elder. "Almost all will be leaving shortly. Each of you is about to begin your soul's great adventure."

"What do you mean almost?" asked Justin, suddenly nervous at a separation from Ashley. He turned to catch a glimpse of her profile as she watched the elder from a few seats away.

"Well, each of you has a special birth path. Some will be leaving sooner than others."

Justin wondered what that really meant. How long would he have to wait to find her. He prayed silently that it would be soon.

Jaron glanced over at Brooke apprehensively. How long would they be separated? Where would they find each other? Brooke attempted a smile, but her stomach was queasy.

The malaise was general. It was in the air. For the first time every member of the class was facing the unknown alone. They had passed through the training together. They had faced hardships and overcome the Human Condition as a team. Now all twenty-five of them were facing the future by themselves.

Élan felt the tension in his right arm as his fingers unconsciously traced the letters on the cover of the manual. He stopped and looked over at Zendar, momentarily wishing they could be born together. He knew it was impossible. Both had already accepted the inevitability of separation. Now they must focus on finding one another in the future.

Elder Em's voice cut through his thoughts. "Élan will go first," he said quietly.

Élan's eyes shot up, searching the elder's eyes for an explanation. "It can't be this soon." The entire class held their breath.

"The time is now."

"Do I really have to go first?"

"You need to be the eldest when the team is born."

"But I'm scared."

"It will be all right. Your mother is expecting you soon," answered the Elder with quiet certainty.

Élan was still hesitant, so the elder continued. "There are beings waiting on the other side to help you, Élan. Although you will be born into the home of a sleeping family, there is a timetable for your awakening. You will be called, and once your awakening begins there will be help for you in your soul's quest to become love in action." Elder Em acknowledged the room. "The plan will unfold according to a very specific timetable for each of you," he said. "Trust the plan."

"I do," Élan answered as he walked to the front of the room with the attention of the class riveted on him. "I really do." His voice was barely audible.

Élan looked down the long row to where his friend was seated. Zendar sprang to his feet and was at Élan's side in an instant. As the two embraced, he whispered, "We'll find each other, my friend." His voice was shaky. "I promise!"

"I need you," Élan answered.

"I need you too, Élan."

"We won't wait very long to find each other, will we?"

"I'll be there soon." Zendar felt as if his heart would break. They had been together for so long. How would he ever make it through the years without him? Who would he share his thoughts and dreams with? He had to strengthen Élan now. "We'll help each other find the real cave down there," he said reassuringly.

Élan nodded bravely. "And Rhea?"

"We'll find her too." Zendar's chest hurt.

"As soon as you're ready." Elder Em's voice was gentle, but they couldn't delay.

"I'm ready." Élan's voice trembled with the inevitable. His eyes were still on Zendar. "Love you, Zen."

"You too." Zendar stepped back away from Élan as he spoke.

"I love all of you too." Élan turned to face the group. Brooke nodded.

"Look for me when you're down there, Élan," called Justin. "I'll be coming in right behind you!"

Élan couldn't help but smile. His friend was ever true to form. He looked at Zendar. There were tears in his friend's eyes.

"Time to turn in your body suit," Elder Em said quietly, snapping his fingers. "Your mother has your real one waiting for you."

Élan's soul-light suddenly shimmered brightly as he awaited the elder's next command. Then realizing that the elder was waiting for him to take the lead, he added, "Could you please tell me what to do next. I'm a little nervous."

"Of course." The elder smiled, sensitive to the moment. "It's time to go now, Élan," he said. "Remember to remember who you are." He bowed his head slightly in the direction of Élan's light. "Go now and God be with you on your life journey." The elder's right hand went up in the gesture of a blessing as Élan's light slowly began to dissolve. A moment later, Zendar was left standing alone with Elder Em in the front of the room.

"Is that it?" Justin whispered, suddenly startled into awareness by the finality of the experience. "Is Élan really gone for good?"

"Élan has passed through the Window of Time," the elder answered quietly.

The gaping silence in the room was staggering as the stark reality hit everyone. This time there was no excitement or enthusiasm. This time there were no familiar crackles and pops of the transmission. This time there was no anticipation of the future. They would not participate with Élan, nor would Élan return.

Zendar's legs were shaking. He looked over at the elder apprehensively. How should he react? He'd never been through anything like this before. He felt as if he needed a script or guidelines of some kind. He was empty, stunned.

Sensing Zendar's dilemma, Elder Em moved toward him. He reached for the young man's shoulder. "He'll be all right," he said. Zendar's eyes searched his face. "And so will you," he added. "It will all work out in its own time, Zendar, I promise."

"I guess it's my turn to work on patience." Zendar smiled slightly at the thought. He'd always been the stronger of the two in that regard, but now somehow he felt lost, insecure.

"We have to go on, Zendar," Elder Em said with a gently apology in his tone. "We don't have a choice."

"I know. I'm sorry, sir." Zendar choked back his feelings. "I thought it would be easy. I thought I was prepared. After all, I knew that birth was coming. I'd almost been looking forward to it. We would all be moving on to fulfill our own life plans.

"But now, facing birth alone, I'm numb." Zendar's eyes were filled with tears. "I can't imagine being without him, sir. We were the best of friends."

Elder Em was tender. "You always will be." He squeezed Zendar's arm affirmingly. "You'll be together again someday," he smiled. "Trust your own inner knowing, Zendar. Don't ever forget who you are."

Zendar's shoulders instantly relaxed as he stared into the elder's soft green eyes. "Oh thank you, sir." He needed to hold onto the future now. It was all he had. Both of his best friends were waiting for him there, beyond the window in another time. He must trust life and the vows that they had all made to find each other someday. "I understand," he said, moving toward his seat.

Elder Em paused as Zendar sat down. The silence in the room was filled with apprehension. "It's your turn now, my friend," Elder Em said, turning his gaze quietly to Justin, who was fidgeting with the binding of his manual.

"I'm not sure I'm ready, Elder Em." Justin's face flushed with nervous anxiety. "Couldn't you send someone else first?"

"You know that there's a timetable, Justin," Elder Em answered. "Your mother's readiness can't be changed."

Justin turned to Ashley, who was sitting next to him. His hand reached across the distance between the chairs, and she took it.

"I won't forget," she said quietly. "We'll find each other down there."

Staring into her eyes, Justin breathed deeply as if to inhale her words. He nodded and released Ashley's hand as he stood and began his slow walk to the front of the room. Zendar watched as their friend turned and faced the group.

"Are you ready, Justin?" Elder Em asked quietly.

"As ready as I'll ever be." Justin nodded, his gaze steadily holding Ashley's eyes.

"Time to turn in your simulated body suit," Elder Em said.

Justin's suit slowly dissolved, and his soul-light soon filled the front of the room.

Zendar watched in rapt fascination, thinking of Élan as he observed the differences in color between the two. He'd never realized the distinction before, but now he was aware of clear variations in color and vibration. Élan's was made up of various shades of violet with gold flecks shimmering through the feathered edges. Justin's light leaned toward shades of blue and green. The distinct differences reminded him momentarily of the jewels in his dream. He knew that each color represented a different energy, and he wondered how each would manifest on Earth.

"Remember to remember who you are, Justin," Elder Em said, raising his hand in acknowledgment. "May your life journey be blessed." And with that,

Justin's light dissolved and Elder Em was left standing in the front of the room alone again.

Zendar soon became lost in thought as Elder Em began moving methodically through the group. One by one each soul came forward and said good-bye to the group. One by one each of them turned in their simulated body suits to disappear beneath the layer of clouds. Zendar's awareness drifted in and out until it came to Jaron's turn.

He held Brooke's hand for a long time before walking bravely to the front of the room. Zendar acknowledged him with a nod, and then he too was gone. Brooke followed right behind, but Zendar knew that it would probably be years before they found each other.

When Ashley's name was called, he smiled at her in an attempt to give her some reassurance. He felt connected to Ashley through Justin, and he silently wished her well as she walked to the front of the room. He watched her departure closely, noticing that her light was blue and violet as she slowly dissolved before his eyes.

Finally the room was empty. Only Zendar and the elder remained.

"Well, Elder Em," Zendar stood and began walking to the front of the room as he had watched so many others do, "it must be my turn." He was definitely ready, having waited through the entire process.

Elder Em was quiet as his student approached.

Zendar stepped to the elder's side. "I'm ready," he said. He was thinking of Élan. The sooner he was born, the sooner he would find him.

"Your destiny is different, Zendar." Elder Em's eyes gazed steadily into his.

"What do you mean? I'm going to be born aren't I?"

"In time."

"In time?"

"You have to wait awhile Zendar. Arrangements for your birth must still be made."

"I'm confused, Elder Em, help me."

"You made a promise when you were on Earth, Zendar."

"I did?"

"You did."

"Oh, of course," Zendar reflected, "the one to Rhea." His face lit up with the memory of Rhea.

"Yes, that one," the elder acknowledged, "And it shifted your destiny."

"How?"

"You promised you'd come back to help her." He paused as he looked into Zendar's deep blue eyes. "A promise is etched in the ethers of eternity," he said. "And now you are bound by your word."

"But how will I ever keep my promise to her?"

"We're working on that right now," Elder Em answered.

"But how?" Zendar couldn't imagine how he

could help her. She would have to be so much older than he when they met. He was completely confused. "Please explain."

"Right now we are in the process of guiding Rhea through her despair," he said. "In time she will meet another man, a special kind of man, one who is deep and sensitive, one who will want to share her journey."

"But what does that have to do with me?" Zendar queried.

"They'll marry and eventually Rhea will have a child."

"Me?" Zendar interrupted. His eyes were wide with amazement. "But if I'm a baby, how will I ever help her?" He couldn't hide his bewilderment.

"The waiting time will be a time of extra preparation for you, Zendar." Elder Em faced his student as he spoke. "You'll have a very special body when you're born," he said. "During the time of waiting you'll stay with me to be trained in the art and application of perfect love."

Zendar was pleased. An extra time apprenticing at the side of Elder Em was more than he'd anticipated. "Will I get to see Raoul again?" he asked, excited at the thought.

"We'll see." The Elder smiled mysteriously as he gestured toward the door.

They left the course room together, and that evening the elder helped Zendar move into his new living quarters. He was to be across the hall from the master during the period of his apprenticeship. The new group of trainees would be coming in a short time, but Zendar would remain near his dear teacher.

That night Zendar slept deeply, tired from the day's events. He prayed for guidance both in the training and in his life to come.

EPILOGUE

Every mother searches her doctor's face in the first moments after birth. Rhea was no exception, but it was not the doctor's face that told the story. Following the baby's cry, there was an instant hush in the birthing room, a silent pall that filled the air around her bed.

"Well?" she asked, beads of perspiration still running down her face from the labor.

"It's a boy," he said, tenderly stroking the feet of the newborn child.

"What's the silence?"

"It's not too bad, Rhea."

"What are you talking about? Where is he?"

"He's here, Rhea. I'm so sorry. Your son's legs didn't form properly early in pregnancy, and he has what we call club feet."

"Please give him to me."

The doctor tenderly handled the child, his little body wrapped in a blanket, to Rhea. She pulled him into her breast, and Rhea's husband, Michael, moved anxiously to her side.

"Leave us alone with him," she said quietly, reaching for Michael's hand.

"We can't do that, Rhea," said the nurse. "But we will give you a few minutes before we take him to the nursery."

Alone with her husband and child, Rhea pulled the blanket away from their newborn's face. Zendar's heart fluttered as he sensed her presence. It was his beloved Rhea. Rhea's eyes filled with tears as she gazed into the dark blue eyes of her firstborn. She looked up at her husband as she stroked the baby's legs. They didn't understand. His legs looked normal.

When the doctor returned with the nurse, Rhea asked him about it.

"Club feet don't show at birth," he said. "The bones are deformed, but it's the feel of the foot that tells the story, Rhea. It'll become more noticeable as he grows. That's when our work begins."

"How bad is it, doctor?" Michael asked.

"We won't know until we view all the X-rays. In most cases we begin casting the child's legs at about three to four months. In a mild case, we may work with him for only a few years. In severe cases, surgery is often required."

"Will he walk?"

"He'll walk. Modern technology is miraculous. It may be a long process, but your son will live a healthy, normal life." He stopped. "We need to take him to the nursery now."

Rhea and Michael thanked the doctor as the nurse gently removed the child from Rhea's breast. As the door closed behind them, Michael reached for Rhea's hand. Like all parents, they had hoped that their child would be perfect. Now they faced the unknown, and they cried quietly together. How could she go back to work in six weeks? How could she leave their son with anyone else? He would need her help. What would the healing process take?

"At least the doctor said he would walk." Michael stroked Rhea's hair. "Let's pray for guidance."

It was late. Michael curled up on the chair to sleep for a few hours. Rhea was exhausted. She called to God for help before falling asleep.

That night she dreamed. A familiar woman with straight dark hair that rested on her shoulders was standing at a distance in the mist. She was wearing a floor-length ivory-colored robe, and as Rhea approached her she saw that the woman was holding a child out to her. As Rhea reached to take him in her arms, she recognized the child's heartbeat as her own. It was her son.

"He is a gift to you, Rhea," said the woman. Her eyes were filled with empathy and love. "He has come to you to fulfill a promise. If you will only surrender to your love for him, the joy that will flow between you will one day lead you out of the world." A soft enigmatic smile gently spread across her face. "One day he will help you find the cave, Rhea."

As the image of the woman faded in the mist, her voice could be heard, beyond the vapory haze . . . "Surrender to your love, Rhea, and your love will take you home . . ."

The next morning Rhea was clear. She called Michael to her side and shared her dream. She spoke of the beautiful being who had come to her twice in her life bearing a message. Michael listened intently as Rhea shared the woman's inspiring words. He was loving and supportive, and they agreed to trust the counsel given in the dream.

The doctor returned sometime later with X-rays in hand. His face was taut. He called it a challenging case. There would be operations and casts. Michael and Rhea held hands. The dream had strengthened them.

"Time will tell," Michael said quietly.

Rhea asked for their son, and the nurse returned with him.

"My precious baby bird," Rhea whispered as she held him in her arms. "You've come to us wounded, but we'll find a way. Someday you'll walk with angels, my son."

"Have you settled on a name?" asked the nurse.

"Zendar," she answered quietly. "I'll call him Zendar . . ."